OTHER BOOKS BY LORIN GRACE

American Homespun Series
Waking Lucy
Remembering Anna
Reforming Elizabeth
Healing Sarah

Artists & Billionaires
Mending Fences
Mending Christmas
Mending Walls
Mending Images
Mending Words
Mending Hearts

Hastings Security
Not the Bodyguard's Baby
Not the Bodyguard's Widow
Not the Bodyguard's Boss
Not the Bodyguard's Princess

Misadventures in Love
Miss Guided
Miss Oriented

Hastings Security 5

THE Not BODYGUARD'S Bride

LORIN GRACE

CURRANT
CREEK PRESS

Cover Design © 2019 Evan Frederickson and LJP Creative Graphics
Photos © iStock

Formatting by LJP Creative
Edits by Eschler Editing

Published by Currant Creek Press
North Logan, Utah
Not the Bodyguard's Bride © 2020 by Lorin Grace

First edition: November 2020
ISBN: 978-1-970148-12-1

to the Swim Ladies
THE BEST EARLY MORNING CHEER TEAM.

THE PROBLEM WITH SOCIAL MEDIA was that everyone knew the truth but believed the lie. Manipulated images were headlined by misleading titles. Algorithms led users to only one side of the story, which was why 30 percent of Alan's job involved sitting in a darkened room with five monitors mounted to his desk. A viral New Year's story in a disreputable journal had Alan filtering through one client's social media for the source of the latest threat. If people could only see how much damage they did to others with uneducated comments, perhaps they'd be more careful posting and reposting without verification.

Alan typed several keywords into a search bot created by Hastings's biggest client, C&O Enterprises' Colin Ogilvie. The program needed ten to fifteen minutes to run, so Alan walked around the office to stretch his muscles. Most of the cubicles sat empty as the personal security team members were elsewhere in Chicago and beyond, doing what they did best.

ZoElle Watson hurried around a corner, her eyes on her phone screen. Alan sidestepped her to avoid a collision. She raised her eyes from her phone. "Sorry, Mr. Alan. I wasn't looking."

"Anything wrong?"

"Someone on Deidre's team has to leave. Family emergency. She needs me as backup."

"Did you change the roster?"

She pinched her lips. Of course she had. She always did. "Yes, and I have Ben filling in for me on Mr. Alex's team."

"Why isn't Ben on D's team?"

"It's an all-female team for September Platt's bridal-gown fitting. Are you okay? You're usually a step ahead of me on this stuff." ZoElle was the only employee in the company's history to work herself up from office receptionist to full bodyguard. None of the other team members would have noticed his slip—the type that only happened around his former client, now coworker.

"Sorry, my head is in the project on my desk."

ZoElle's phone beeped. Standing this close in the quiet office, he could hear the voice in her earpiece. "Elle? Are you coming?"

She started walking as she answered. "Leaving the office now."

No one would ever suspect when they'd met over a year ago that she'd been sitting, curled up on her kitchen floor, practically catatonic. A victim of more than social media. The image was one of the few from his job that haunted him. The incident proved how much damage social media could do. He tried to keep the picture deep in the back of his mind. It didn't help that ZoElle kept bringing the incident back up. Like a few weeks ago, she had gone on another nationally televised talk show with Zoe Wilson-Gooding discussing the harm media, social and traditional, had caused in their lives.

The image in his mind proved why ZoElle wasn't ready to be a personal security team leader. Falling apart when things got tough wouldn't cut it. Their client's safety had to be the priority. He wouldn't deny she had more fortitude than most people he knew. Not a gender issue either. If he'd seen a man as broken, Alan would block his promotion too.

2

Sometimes punching someone in the face was cathartic, even if that someone was a six-foot sparring dummy. Mortimer's plastisol rubber nose flattened well beyond the manufacturer's recommendations. Elle gave him one more punch, releasing her frustration over Mr. Alan trying to block her promotion test. She wasn't supposed to know he'd tried to reschedule her test for another six months. The interview portion with Mr. Alex wasn't supposed to end early either.

"Miss Watson, please move to the next station." Jethro Hastings's deep voice cut through her concentration.

Mr. Alan and Mr. Adam waited at the other end of the sparring mat. Elle approached Jethro, removing the boxing gloves from her last test and wiping the perspiration from her hands. From what she'd heard, once they started hand-to-hand combat, she had ninety seconds to take Alan to the mat—a feat she'd accomplished more than once in the past year with every one of his brothers and one actual threat. The problem was that Alan not only knew what moves to expect, he doubted her abilities.

He'd never told her face-to-face, but she suspected it, and the conversation she'd overheard that morning verified it. Alan had seen her at her lowest during the worst week of her life—a week she would never forget. A week, with the help of good friends and an excellent therapist, she had overcome. She didn't need six more months to prepare. Elle was ready even if Alan wasn't.

Mr. Adam, the oldest of the Hastings brothers, stood in the center of the mat holding an index card. "Miss Watson, you have five minutes to complete your task. They have captured you and your principal. Your hands are zip-tied, as are your feet. There is a guard outside your door. You must get your principal to the red X on the far side of the mat. "Since the real-life version would most likely have a wall between you and your abductor, Mr. Alan will wear noise canceling headphones until he hears you or you cross the white line—in which case you will be in the same room with him. Deidre will act as your principal. She may cooperate but not aid. Do you understand your assignment?"

When was this added to the test? No one had warned her about a role-play. "Yes. I do."

Deidre sat on the floor against the wall, hands and feet zip-tied, head bowed. Mr. Adam handed Elle the blazer she'd worn to work. "Put this on. You would have been on duty when abducted."

As sweaty as she was, the jacket would need dry cleaning. There must be some advantage to having her suit coat, or the Hastings wouldn't have included it as part of the test. Elle put it on.

Mr. Adam held up a zip tie. Elle crossed her wrists and flexed.

"Nice try. Wrists together." Mr. Adam put on the restraint. As she sat down, she realized that other than her phone, they had removed nothing from her pockets. Mr. Adam zip-tied her feet together, complicating her escape. The fastest way to remove wrist restraints was to raise her hands above her head and bring her arms down as fast as she could—only she had to be standing for the maneuver. Sitting didn't work for her.

Mr. Adam walked to the side and tapped his phone. "Start now."

Deidre looked up then. "They will kill us. What are we going to do?"

"Deidre, look at me." Elle repeated the instructions until Deidre met her eyes. "We will get out of here, but I need you to stay calm. Can you reach into my pocket? I need you to find my pen."

Deidre and Elle maneuvered until Deidre retrieved a pen with the Hastings logo.

"Place it in my hands with the clicker up."

Deidre complied. Elle bit off the clicker, revealing a miniature flathead screwdriver. She rotated the pen and stuck the flathead in the zip ties locked on her feet, releasing them. Elle set the pen on the floor, then stood and used a slamming motion to break the bonds on her hands. Deidre gasped.

"Just a moment and I'll have you out." Elle scooped up the pen and used the screwdriver to jimmy the locks on Deidre's bonds.

"We have one guard out there. When I say, I need you to run as fast as you can to the red X while I distract him. Don't worry about me."

Deidre stood.

"How well do you run in those heels?" Since Deidre rarely wore heels, they must also be part of the test.

"Not well."

"Give them to me." Elle checked over her shoulder to make sure Mr. Alan wore protective sparring gear. She kept one shoe in her hand and the pen in the other. "Be as quiet as you can, and when I say run, make like an Olympic gold medalist."

Deidre nodded. Elle led them across the mat to the white line Mr. Alan guarded.

"I can't do this." Deidre pulled back. "He'll kill us. I know he will."

Elle made eye contact with Deidre again. "You can do this. Anyone who can rock these shoes can do anything. Ready?"

Deidre nodded.

"On three. One, two…three!" Elle gave Deidre a push as they crossed the line. Elle whirled to face Mr. Alan and brought the stiletto heel of the shoe down on his helmet with a yell. "Run!"

Mr. Alan moved to grab Elle's arm, but she brought the pen around to his side, stabbing the foam jacket. Mr. Alan looked down. Elle swept his leg as Deidre had taught her, spinning as she did. Using his momentum, she brought him to the floor and pinned him. "Run for the X, Deidre!" Her pretend principal complied.

"Complete!" yelled Jethro Hastings.

Elle brushed herself off and turned to Mr. Adam.

"Four minutes, thirty-six seconds. Good job." Mr. Adam held out his hand.

"A screwdriver?" Mr. Alan came up behind her with the pen she'd dropped on the mat as she'd pinned him. "And you put a hole in the vest."

5

"Better than putting a hole in you."

"Clean up and report to my office for your scores." Jethro Hastings's face failed to betray his thoughts.

Deidre followed Elle into the dressing room. "I wish I'd thought of using the shoes when I took this test."

"Why didn't anyone warn me? I thought this was the normal 'endurance, then spar' test we do for recertifications." Elle gathered her things and headed off to take a quick shower.

Deidre followed but stayed outside the shower area, shouting over the echo of the spray. "It's top secret. More to see how you react under pressure when keeping your principal in mind. Say you hadn't taken the time to calm me down. I could have started shouting and screaming loud enough to alert the guard."

"Can you find my pen? Alan took it, and I'd like it back."

"Did you make the pen yourself?"

"I modified it."

"Not how I expected you to use the pen when you asked me to help you with it." Deidre's voice trailed off.

Elle turned off the shower and dried her face. The adrenaline was wearing off. "How is married life treating you?"

"I can't believe we've been married for a month already. Coming home to Liam is so much nicer than I expected. He goes out of his way to make sure he doesn't remind me of my ex, which he never could in a thousand years." Deidre stuffed several items from her locker into her duffel.

"Any plans to jump ship and work for Dermot Security?"

"No, I like Hastings, and keeping our work life separate is good for us. We'd like to start a family, and I don't want to miss my kids' first steps, so for now I'll stay with Hastings until I do a temporary retirement."

"I should thank you again for all the help you've been this past year. I never thought I would be able to take my final tests this fast."

"You're a quick and dedicated learner. I hope they promote you."

"Because I am good or so you don't feel bad retiring in the next year or so?"

"Both!" Deidre laughed. "I'd better get up there so I can put in my vote. See you in a few."

Elle reapplied her makeup and twisted her hair into a bun. Not daring to dawdle longer, she turned out the lights. Time to face Hastings management. Would she start the new year as Hastings's newest senior bodyguard?

"This isn't authorized equipment." Alan set ZoElle's pen on his father's desk. "What is she doing with it?"

Alex picked up the pen. "I assume she's been improvising. I don't think we've ever had an applicant or trainee who has studied so much. The zipper-bag thing she did with Kimberly's letter last summer was brilliant."

Alan grudgingly agreed. He thought about how the team had worried a birthday card from Kimberly's deceased husband might be poisoned and ZoElle had placed the envelope in a large zipper bag with a plastic knife, allowing them to open and read the card without risking contamination. He wished he thought of nonstandard ideas like she did.

Jethro continued. "I've been impressed again and again by her out-of-the-box thinking. The entire month she was on my team last summer, she was always studying. She must have gone through a hundred zip ties practicing ways to get out, which she'd found on the internet."

"Let me see the pen." Deidre Ross-Dermot held out her hand. "I need to get her to make me one."

"Even if she passed today's test, she isn't ready." Alan sat down in a padded chair, crossed his arms, and looked around the room. They didn't get it. They hadn't seen ZoElle cowering behind the kitchen counter, tears running down her face. She wasn't a protector. She needed protecting.

His dad leaned forward in his chair. "She has surpassed my expectations at every turn. We've been quiet while you put her through a more detailed training than most of our bodyguards get. Alan, I don't think she is the one who isn't ready. She'll be up here any moment. If you can't celebrate her promotion, I suggest you go to your office."

Dad was right. He couldn't be here.

Alan crossed the office and left, feeling the weight of everyone's eyes on him. Only six more months, then she'd be ready—maybe. Many of their other bodyguards took two or three years to get this promotion. They didn't need to rush ZoElle. Letting her prove herself wasn't a bad thing.

2

THE PAGE OF THE PARENTING magazine blurred in front of Elle as she sat in the pediatrician's office waiting for her principal's exit. Not much had changed since her promotion other than she didn't rotate through details as often. Her primary responsibility was to the wife and children of one of their biggest clients. Since the children were under the age of three, doctors' offices, parks, museums, and short shopping trips consumed most of her working hours. The biggest complication of her day was when a child she guarded decided it was time to hug their polyester-pants-wearing shadow and wrapped their sticky arms around her legs. It had become a running joke that the bodyguard's pants were as good as a washcloth, as rarely did a toddler dive in for a hug unless covered with food or another sticky substance. And homemade slime wasn't easy to get out.

Elle turned the page and scanned the room. She was the only person without a child nearby. A mother with an infant in a carseat carrier gave Elle the stink eye. Hoping to look less conspicuous, Elle checked her phone. A new message on the Hastings app lit up the screen.

Urgent Meeting 4 p.m.—Mr. Hastings's Office.

The message was also sent to Mr. Alan.

Elle replied with her acceptance. A meeting with Jethro would either mean a new assignment or trouble. Unfortunately, trouble was more likely.

Alan had been distant since her promotion. For the last several days, he'd assigned her the undemanding jobs and kept her on desk duties. Maybe Mr. Hastings had noticed how their early camaraderie had developed into a strained silence. Melanie Hastings had been around the office more since Andrew had left for California. The mom of the Hastings clan missed nothing. She'd know Elle was actively avoiding Alan. Anything to keep her crush at bay.

She hadn't heeded the warnings a year and a half ago not to fall in love with her rescuer. The insta-crush had faded only to be replaced by something more. Even at Alan's worst, which she'd had plenty of opportunities to see, she still wanted nothing more than to knock some sense into him and get him to see her. And then kiss him until he felt the chemistry too. How could he miss it? The air all but sizzled around them anytime they were in the same room.

Even his family made the occasional comment about a future for the two of them. Perhaps it was better that she leave Hastings Security. Simon Dermot's firm was recruiting female bodyguards. Or she could go back to her former career. She'd been moonlighting, and one of Hastings's clients had offered to hire her more than once. The lure of multiple computer monitors filled her every time she had to stand guard outside a preschool music hour. But her programming career wasn't where her heart was...she could always go back to programming after a few years of being a bodyguard. Personal security wasn't the type of career people stayed in until retirement age, not to mention retirement due to injury.

Elle scanned the waiting room again and checked the Hastings app. Her client was still in the examining room, where she'd been for the last fifty minutes. Proof money didn't always buy privileges, like jumping to the head of the line in a doctor's office.

Elle opened her notes app and typed in a few thoughts regarding her resignation. She'd need to talk with Dermott Security about a position first. Was it best to resign before or after she talked with Mr. Hastings today?

When the door to the examining room opened, Elle stood to walk her client and crying daughter out. The new job could wait for another day.

Alan's phone pinged, reminding him of the meeting in his father's office. He'd spent part of the afternoon trying to figure out why Jethro wanted to see ZoElle and him. He was the last one to the meeting. "Mom, what are you doing here?"

Melanie Hastings smiled. "Nice to see you too, Alan."

Alan took the only seat left—next to ZoElle.

Jethro sat behind his desk. He turned his monitor so everyone could see a photo of a couple. A blue-eyed blonde leaned against a lean, olive-skinned male, her hand resting on his shoulder and showing off a large diamond engagement ring. "We received a rather interesting request from a firm in Dallas we've worked with on occasion. Cassie Evans, an oil heiress, is getting married. She is adamant she not have bodyguards on her honeymoon, which is an impossibility, even with her unassuming lifestyle."

Alan tried to place the name. "Evans…didn't their son marry one of the Art House women and go to Haiti?"

"Yes. Kyle Evans married Araceli Williams. They are back in Texas now as Haiti has been too dangerous for Americans for months. Anyhow, Cassie is the older of the sisters. According to what they gave me, she is a licensed RN and is on the board of several Dallas-area hospitals. She is marrying a doctor who recently returned from working in Africa."

"When's the wedding?" asked ZoElle.

"Valentine's Day."

Melanie shook her head. "That's the day Adam and September are getting married. We can't possibly help."

"The job doesn't start until a day later, when Miss Evans and her husband board a fourteen-day cruise through the Panama Canal."

Alan leaned forward at his father's announcement. "A cruise? What happened to billionaires renting yachts?"

"She's an Evans—one of those families who tries to look normal." Alan didn't need to have his father explain further. The Evanses were third-generation oil money. When Kyle Evans married two years ago, they'd kept security to a minimum. Abbie had attended their nuptials in Boston.

ZoElle looked from one person to another. "Mrs. Hastings, I'm missing something here."

"Elle, you need to call us Jethro and Melanie." Melanie smiled in a motherly way. "Deah Evans is the daughter of an oil tycoon. She's overseen the family's charitable interests since her late teens. Somehow, she's created a rather normal life for the family as they strive not to live an extravagant lifestyle. So far, her children have followed in her footsteps. Almost all the bodyguards the family uses daily are undercover. Sometimes the Evanses aren't even aware of the protection provided by Mrs. Evans's father. Finding security Miss Evans won't recognize on a cruise has stretched their firm to the limit."

Alan nodded, not surprised that his mother knew the assignment particulars. She had one of the best minds in the industry for strategizing security and often freelanced her services.

"Oh, so they need undercover bodyguards?" asked ZoElle.

Jethro produced a layout of the ship. "According to the call I received this morning, Miss Evans has reluctantly agreed to allow two bodyguards on their excursions to foreign ports. As you can imagine, no one is comfortable with this plan, so they've contracted with us to fill in the gaps."

"A standard cruise ship has more cameras on board than rolls of toilet paper. Outside the rooms, both guests and crew are constantly on camera." Alan's eyes fell to the floor plans. "What do they need from us?" As soon as he said the words, he knew.

Melanie beamed. "Miss Evans and her new husband will stay in the ship's premier luxury stateroom. The Dallas firm contracted for two other nearby suites. They want another set of newlyweds and an older couple to occupy those rooms. Your father and I are going to celebrate our forty-fifth wedding anniversary a few years early, and you two will—"

ZoElle gasped, her cheeks flushing red.

Alan shook his head. "Us? Pretend to be married? Use someone else. Deidre and Liam or Tonie and Ben. Aren't they still dating?" The latest co-worker romance started at the same time and on the same job as his youngest brother's relationship with an actress. Tonie and Ben had been working with separate teams for months now.

"Deidre is coordinating security for Adam and September's honeymoon, and Dermott Security is undergoing transition. It's unlikely we could get Liam for a fifteen-day assignment. Ben is in Japan with clients." Jethro shook his head.

"How can I go undercover? I was on the cover of *Gossip Today* with Zoe and Nick Gooding just two weeks ago." ZoElle's blush faded.

Mom opened a folder. "I've been combing through the media, and I think the answer is you don't go undercover. You use your names and backstory. You met Alan when Nick Gooding sent him to protect you from the media a year ago last October. There are several photos showing Alan in your vicinity acting as a bodyguard. Most everything in the media, including last week's *Gossip Today*, has been a rehashing of the original television interviews, looking at the #metoo movement from the harm media is doing—which is ironic. No one has followed up on where you are now. With Alan's help, you've kept your current career under wraps. Even the fact that you live in Chicago only comes up a couple times."

"Some reporters have done some snooping, but I don't think anyone has followed me around enough to realize where I work. Zoe and Nick Gooding have the high profile. I'm along because without the attack on me, the story doesn't exist." ZoElle's voice was devoid of emotion, the same as when she'd come out of those dreaded interviews. Alan couldn't understand why she continued to grant interviews about how a misreporting of her rape had ended up as headline news, falsely accusing a New York billionaire and dredging up old news about his current wife. Yes, it was helping media responsibility, but from what he'd seen during his last foray into social media, most of the human race didn't realize they were part of the problem.

Melanie cleared her throat. "We'll have to stage your wedding in the middle of Adam and September's in order to pull this off."

"Wait. Why do we need a wedding?" asked Alan.

Jethro leaned forward. "You don't need a wedding. You need photos."

"Why?"

Melanie rested a hand on Alan's shoulder. "Every bride has photos of her wedding on her phone and all over social media. On the night of Adam's rehearsal, we are going to have a little photo shoot at the church. Then, when you show everyone your photos, you'll say you decided you couldn't wait, and after your brother left, you two had a small ceremony of your own so as to not detract from your brother's special day. The cruise was a wedding present from Abbie. Who, by the way, has already agreed to let Elle go through the magazine's warehouse and find a wedding dress to borrow."

"Wait, you've talked to my sister but not me? Abbie doesn't work here anymore." Alan tried not to let his anger show, but his voice was sharper than he wanted it to be.

"I needed to make arrangements for Harmony during your brother's honeymoon. I can't bring a grandbaby when I am celebrating my anniversary." Mom pulled out another folder. "Cruise packing list."

Alan read the paper, which was specific enough to include the pairs and colors of socks he'd need.

ZoElle made a small, strangled sound in her throat. "I don't own many of these things."

Mom smiled. "You won't use some of these things, but the lingerie will come in handy if you get a nosy housekeeper in your room. Abbie said she could pull the lingerie from the warehouse as well. Alan, do you need your sis—"

"No. I'll take care of the list myself." Alan's face burned. He didn't dare look up. The packing list included several things a new husband might want on board but which were inappropriate for a working situation, even if their purpose was to keep the ship's crew from getting too curious. "Is there anything else?"

Melanie checked her folder. "I'll email you the times for the photo shoots. Abbie is taking care of those. She's been itching to do more photography. Do you two have any photos together?"

"No." At least not that Alan would claim. There might be one or two from the couple of family events ZoElle had attended buried deep in his phone. Or from last year's inter-company competition, when his brothers had signed ZoElle to partner with him on the two-person obstacle course and the three-legged race, where they'd placed second. No one had beat Liam and Deidre in the event since they'd trounced Alex's and Abbie's records.

Melanie wrote a note on a legal pad. Unlike the rest of the family, she refused to keep her notes in her phone.

Jethro's chair squeaked. "There is one other problem. If you are going to pull off the newlywed thing, you'll need to find a way to be friends again. I haven't heard the two of you laughing for weeks now."

Alan nodded.

ZoElle studied him before turning to his father. "We'll try."

Dad looked like he was going to say something but then shook his head. "Melanie and I have things to discuss. Tomorrow, you'll both be in here working on the details. Elle, does your team have any outings not in the app? The schedule seems more quiet than usual."

"No, little Miss Crawford has an ear infection, so the Crawfords canceled everything on their schedule not work related. Mrs. Ogilvie is going only to her art studio. The regular driver and on-site personnel should be adequate."

"Good. See you two tomorrow."

Alan followed ZoElle out. He should say something, but his mind was blank.

"See you tomorrow." ZoElle waved and disappeared into the maze of cubicles.

Alan returned to his office. Out of habit, he checked each of the monitors on his desk. According to the screens, everything was perfectly quiet. Obviously, his new assignment hadn't been entered yet. There was nothing normal about pretending to be married to the one woman he avoided. Alan spun around and headed for the gym. Maybe one of his brothers would be there and they could spar. He'd do anything to get rid of the feeling growing inside him since Dad had announced his assignment.

ELLE HELD UP THE PINK sundress. "I think the blue one is better. Are you sure I need all these clothes?"

Abbie laughed. "You are on a two-week cruise. You'll have dinner, dancing, shows, and long walks on the deck, not to mention excursions."

"I think you're having too much fun with my work assignment." Elle held up a black swimming suit.

"Not that suit. The fabric reacts with chlorine and becomes translucent in water."

She hurried to choose a different swimsuit. "Why would someone make such a thing?"

"Preston and I had a lot of fun with the prototype and the matching men's suit in our private pool. I don't think it would be appropriate for your 'honeymoon.'"

"The lingerie isn't either," she said over a dozen bits of colored lace she didn't dare hold up to see how they looked. As much as she loved Abbie as a friend, Elle didn't need the teasing. The assignment was difficult enough without blushing constantly.

"True, but you won't be using it. It's just for show. Everything's handwash, so rinse out a piece or two every couple days. That way the housekeepers won't be able to tell tales about the weird honeymooners who never take the fun things out of the drawers. This one has a flaw, so you can strategically rip it and leave it in the trash can."

"You realize Alan will turn red the moment he sees any of this." Not to mention she would die on the spot.

Abbie's grin was pure evil. "I only wish I could see his reaction. Speaking of—let's get you down to the photo studio. We have a year of dating history to re-create."

Elle followed Abbie downstairs. "When I met you, I didn't think you cared much for fashion."

"I'd been married about three or four months then? I didn't care much. However, this is Preston's business and world. My mother-in-law pointed out if I showed up at an event wearing something comfortable and worn, people wouldn't respect my taste or, in turn, Preston's. So I took a crash course in the fashion world. Fortunately, the Harmon empire includes other types of magazines, so it isn't all about fashion. At home I wear my old comfortable clothes. But with four brothers, I missed out on the girl dress-up time, and I discovered I love it. It's most fun when I can share."

Alan awaited them near the back wall of the photo studio.

Abbie gave him a hug. "Let's see what you brought." She dug through his clothes. "Do you own a shirt without a work or sports-team logo?"

Alan held up his button-downs.

"Work." Abbie tsked and shook her head.

"Usually when I am out of the office, it's between work events, so this is what I'd be wearing."

Abbie tapped her chin. "These will work for the early dating photos. I'll go find something for the engagement and later dating." She shook her head. "Ten outfits and only the parka looks like you know how to do something besides work."

The photographer joined them. "I want to shoot in chronological order so each photo looks like you are moving closer, falling more in love. Some shots will be staged selfies. They can't be too beautiful or they won't be believable. May I have your phones?"

Alan glared at his sister. "I thought you were taking the photos."

"Green-screen work and positioning models are beyond what I can do. But I'll stick around. I need an afternoon without three little boys learning to say *Mama*."

"Why do you need our phones?" asked Elle.

"I need to see what types of photos you take. If you take a selfie every morning before you go to work, we have to do these before your dates."

"I'm not a big selfie fan." Elle opened her photo gallery and handed the photographer her phone.

"This is good. You have a few of Mr. Alan in here and of you interacting with his family. When was this taken?" The photographer showed her one from a Hastings work party where she and Alan had won the three-legged race.

"First part of September."

The photographer held out his hand for Alan's. Alan handed his over.

"You met when?"

"A year and a half ago in October." Alan didn't give the exact date, although he must have known it as she surely did. No one forgot the second-worst day of their life, especially when it was in the same week as the first worst day. Good thing she didn't need to show photos from before she met Alan. Her life had been so different, so reclusive, so quiet.

The photographer held the phone up to show Alan a photo. "I'd recommend you delete this."

Elle saw enough of the baggy sweatshirt to recognize the photo Alan had taken just minutes after they'd met. She knew the photo was attached to her old client file. Why would he have kept it on his phone?

The photographer scrolled through Elle's phone and grinned. "These are good. They show your personality. We'll begin your romance in October—a stroll in the park with the leaves falling. Go change into sweaters or sweatshirts—what you would wear outside on a sunny fall afternoon."

Over the next hour, Elle got a lesson on why one should never trust a photo as four months of dating history could be packed into dozens of photos.

Twelve changes of clothes later, Alan buttoned a blue plaid shirt over a pale-blue T-shirt—another outfit Abbie had brought him, ignoring his ability to choose his clothes.

His sister covered her mouth to squelch a laugh. "Unbutton the shirt and let it hang open. Remind me to go through your cruise attire."

"No way."

Abbie straightened his collar. "It's for your own good. You are supposed to be the happy newlywed, not the why-did-she-marry-him guy. Here's your ring. Remember, the ring is on loan to Hastings."

"Do we have to video the proposal?"

"No. You don't have to say the words. You'll live."

Following the photographer's instructions, Alan went through the motions of proposing in front of the green screen.

"Good. Good. Now, kiss the girl!"

Alan froze. ZoElle's eyes widened.

There had to be a way out of this. He wasn't ready.

Abbie smirked. "What's wrong? Haven't you ever kissed a girl before?" His sister knew full well he hadn't dated as much as their brothers had. And it may have been more than two years since he'd kissed a girl. Unless he counted Harmony's slobbery baby kisses.

Alan brought a hand up to ZoElle's face and brushed his thumb over her lips, resting it in the center. He brought his face close to hers and kissed his thumb.

The photographer stepped from behind his camera. "No. This is not a high school drama class. She doesn't have cooties. This is the love of your life. Kiss her so I believe it!"

How? He'd never kissed a girl with someone watching. Well, when he'd known about it. Abbie and Alex had apparently been spying on him in high school on his first kiss.

"Alan." Abbie stomped over to them. "Take Elle in your arms and do a half twist so your back is to the camera. Elle, put your hands in his hair and pull him close. Touch your noses together, and no one will know you aren't kissing."

"Will that work?" asked ZoElle.

"It will if my oaf of a brother will lose the rod stuck up his spine."

Alan didn't want to force ZoElle into a kiss. "Are you okay with this?"

She laid her hand over his heart. "Alan, when we took this job, I knew there would be public kissing involved. In private, I know you will respect me. You aren't forcing me to do anything unnecessary to my role and nothing against my will."

"You sure? No flashbacks?"

"Positive. Now, let's touch noses and get this over with before it becomes more awkward."

Abbie left them. Alan performed the twist and dip maneuver as Abbie instructed. The odd warmth that usually came anytime he touched ZoElle off the sparring mat filled him. Neither of them closed their eyes. The variations in ZoElle's eyes reflected blue today—like an exotic gemstone rather than the soft clouds normally there. Not that he noticed her eyes. He was just observant—part of the job and all. Or so he'd been telling himself for the last several months.

"Next!" yelled the photographer. "Elle, I want you to put your hands on his shoulder and look into his eyes. You are thinking about standing on tiptoe and kissing him again."

As they followed instructions, Alan continued to puzzle out her eye color when the gems became sparks.

"Elle, up on your toes. That's it. Closer. Now kiss."

ZoElle's lips touched his, then disappeared as she dropped down to her heels.

More. He needed more. But it was exactly what Alan had tried to avoid. He hadn't missed the not-so-subtle prodding of his siblings over the last year or ZoElle's wide-eyed admiration the first weeks after they'd met. No matter how many times he told himself a relationship with a client could never be, his siblings and the chemistry he felt around ZoElle contradicted him. This honeymoon would be the longest two weeks of his life.

Alan turned to the photographer. "We are done here." Without looking back, Alan left the studio.

"Your sister said you walked out of the photo shoot." Mom didn't look up from her computer.

"Tattletale."

"So you didn't stomp out of the studio like a petulant child?"

"I didn't stomp." Alan hadn't stomped for years. He'd walked purposefully.

Mom lowered the screen of her laptop. "I thought you and Elle were friends, but you've been treating her like a pariah ever since her promotion. Come to think of it, you avoided her most of last fall. What's up?"

"Nothing."

His mom raised an eyebrow and frowned—Momspeak for "I know you are lying. You know you are lying. Confess now because I am thinking of a consequence you will not like."

"You know, same thing Andrew claimed was the problem with the family. Work and personal lives mixing. Only now he's part of it. First Abbie and her client, then Adam and his. Alex and Andrew after that. Do you realize the laughingstock we are? We used to be the grade-A Hastings or Jethro's crew. Now, all anyone talks about is the hasty Hastings and their marriages. ZoElle was my client. The secretary thing was a temporary gig to help her get established in a new city. Now she's a bodyguard. That wasn't supposed to happen. There's supposed to be distance."

"Should I give you lecture 328?"

"Not everything is black and white. Not every rule is set in stone."

"It's the same lecture I've been giving to you since you were eleven. Yes, in general, you shouldn't date clients. But Elle hasn't been a client in well over a year. And like most law-enforcement agencies, we ask for notification of relationships so we don't endanger a team. That's why Deidre is staying with our firm now that she's married and why Ben and Tonie don't work on the same team."

"Why did you pair ZoElle with me?"

"We need the honeymooners to be convincing. To be honest, your friendship had a bit of spark to it."

Every one of his siblings had made at least one comment about his friendship with ZoElle. "We've kept our relationship professional."

"Which is one reason we chose you two. Say I put you and Deidre together. No one in a hundred years would believe you were newlyweds, even though you are good friends."

"Deidre is Liam Dermot's wife."

"Can you imagine kissing Deidre?"

"No! Liam would kill me."

Mom laughed. "Liam would appreciate your response. The fact is there is no way two undercover bodyguards can go on a two-week honeymoon and not be seen at least holding hands and kissing from time to time. The photographer was right in asking for the kissing photos, which was when you left, if my source was correct."

"Mom, ZoElle kissed me."

Mom nodded but didn't comment. It was one of those annoying tactics moms learned from Mother Nature.

"It was the kind of kiss five-year-olds give when they get married on the playground. Not even a real kiss."

"And?"

Alan felt his cheeks flame. How had he gotten into this conversation with his mother? "I don't know. I'm afraid I could lose my focus on this job. I can't be another hasty Hastings."

Melanie pulled out a legal pad. "I am not being a nosy mother. Since I am a paid consultant for Hastings Security, I need to ask you some questions."

He knew what was coming. "I'd rather do this with Dad."

"Do you see yourself keeping your relationship professional in private?"

"Of course. You know I would. I will not take advantage of any woman because we are sharing a honeymoon suite. Especially not ZoElle. Not after what she's endured." Her attacker plead guilty for rape and attempted voluntary manslaughter and was serving twenty years—not long enough in Alan's option.

"Prior to this assignment, have you thought of dating Elle?"

Careful phrasing meant he didn't have to lie. There was a moment after that kiss…"No. We are coworkers, and she was my principal. I am not crossing lines."

"Have the two of you discussed your expectations and how you'll handle public moments?"

"No." Sitting across from ZoElle in a conference room and discussing the type of kisses and places to touch would be so awkward. Over the last few years, he'd negotiated a couple such meetings between bodyguards on special assignments.

"I think you need one. Who do you want as the facilitator?"

Not his family. That would intimidate ZoElle. "She should choose."

"Fine. I'll ask her and set the meeting up for Friday. The two of you don't have much time to get this figured out. How are you coming with the other details?"

"Colin Ogilvie has been designing microcommunications devices. He is trying to put them into jewelry. The problem with a cruise is we won't always have a good reason to have our phones with us all the time."

"The camera is the best reason to keep a phone on you. At least you have pockets, women's fashion often doesn't have pockets when you need them." Melanie patted her own pockets.

"That's what Abbie told me, which was why I asked Colin about jewelry devices. He says he's been wanting to create something for Candace anyway. Speaking of which—I need to email him back." It was the best excuse he could come up with for returning to his office.

FIFTEEN MINUTES TILL ONE OF the most awkward meetings of Elle's life—this might even trump her first appearance on network television. Discussing the media missteps of reporting her assault was probably easier than discussing with Alan how many seconds a public kiss should last and whether he should call her snookums in public.

Melanie's invitation to choose the moderator for the expectations meeting left Elle trying to guess who would put Alan and her at ease. Expectations meetings didn't happen often, and she'd only ever read about them. The problem was that half of her choices for moderators had the last name Hastings. Jethro, Melanie, Adam, Alex, Abbie (now Harmon), and Andrew. Andrew had been the easiest to cut from her list as he was in California.

In the end, she'd chosen someone outside of the agency, surprising Melanie with the choice. The wife of the billionaire who had paid for Elle's security hadn't been on her boss's radar. When Elle discovered Zoe Wilson-Gooding would be in town for the weekend for an event hosted by her cousin, she knew she'd found the perfect person. She'd sat through dozens of uncomfortable meetings with Zoe at her side. Outside of her therapist, Zoe knew more details about that terrible week than anyone on the planet.

Melanie okayed the meeting. As far as Elle knew, Alan hadn't said a word about her unusual choice of facilitator.

Unable to sit, Elle went to the restroom as an excuse to move. To her shock, Zoe exited one of the stalls holding a tissue to her lips. She held up a hand to stave off Elle's question, then rinsed out her mouth. "If you so much as hint to my husband that you even thought I worshiped the porcelain goddess in the Hastings restroom, I'll—" Zoe ran back into the stall.

Elle hurried to her desk and pulled out the emergency kit she'd made for her pregnant clients. She returned to the bathroom in time to find Zoe rinsing out her mouth again.

"Here's an emergency bag with ginger candy, peppermints, soda crackers, ginger snaps, and a new toothbrush."

"Your bag? You aren't…?" Zoe raised a brow.

"No, but I've had two clients who are, or were. I made up a few of these bags for emergencies. Doesn't Nick know?"

"He knows and is driving me crazy being overprotective. The flight was a bit bumpy, and my morning sickness hits in the afternoons more often than not. I think this baby is trying to lure me into believing I'm fine before he lashes out at me."

Elle covered her mouth to hide a laugh.

"Laugh all you want. I used to laugh. Karma loves misery." Zoe dug through the kit and pulled out the toothbrush and unwrapped it.

"I think we've both had enough misery for a lifetime. There must be a better theory regarding morning sickness. I hope it doesn't have to do with reading romance books…I'll be doomed." The comment earned a smile.

Zoe finished brushing her teeth. "We'd better go. As I remember, Mr. Alan is a stickler for punctuality."

Elle showed Zoe to the small back conference room.

Melanie Hastings was there with Alan. She waited until everyone took their seats. "I'm not staying. I'm here to make sure everyone knows a recording of this meeting will be kept for internal use. I need you to agree on record. Mrs. Zoe Gooding?"

"Yes."

"ZoElle Watson?"

"Yes."

"Alan Hastings?"

"Yes."

"This recording is intended for internal use only, in case of a dispute. Mrs. Gooding, if you will follow the script." Melanie shut the door behind her as she left.

Zoe studied the screen of the tablet at her seat. "You both filled out questionnaires. Your answers agree on hand-holding in public. Alan may put his hand on Elle's back when socially necessary, specifically ushering her when dancing, etc. Elle may put her hand on Alan's shoulder, back, or chest as necessary, no restrictions."

No surprises there. Elle avoided looking at Alan, knowing what was coming next.

"Kissing. You both agreed to open mouth, no tongue. Good choice for public kissing. Elle, you blush easily, right?"

Elle felt the warmth rush to her cheeks. "I blush even when talking about it."

The dimple on Alan's cheek appeared, as it often did when he suppressed a smile.

"Use the blush. Embarrassment gives Alan an excuse to quickly break off kisses. If necessary, bury your face in his chest or shoulder. I don't see that kind of touch on the list. Mr. Alan, are you comfortable with that move? Nick and I used it in public when we were dating and first married. Usually I was trying not to laugh. Hiding my face satisfied the demand for us to kiss, and it kept things private. Sometimes our lips wouldn't even touch before I ducked away."

Alan cleared his throat. "ZoElle may hide her face as she thinks is necessary."

Elle peeked at Alan. His voice was stiffer and more formal than usual.

"Hugging: Alan, you don't have any restrictions. Elle, you left yours blank."

"I'm not sure how to explain this. Certain types of hugs are triggers for me. Zoe, will you let me demonstrate? Or do you have hugging triggers?"

"Not from Nick, and I don't think you would set them off."

Alan looked from one woman to the other, his brow pinched.

Elle focused on Zoe. "Even in a self-defense class or on the mat, a certain angle or patterns of touch makes me freeze for a second. I know from the gym mirror that a flash of fear crosses my face. Standard side and front hugs are fine. It's the hugs from behind that"—Elle searched for a word—"trigger me."F

Elle stood behind Zoe. "I wish I was a bit taller than you."

Zoe crouched down an inch. Mindful of Zoe's condition, Elle hurried. "Side hug turning into a back hug with the arm looped around my neck. One arm around my waist pulling me against a chest, especially if I don't know where the other hand is."

Alan nodded, and Elle stepped back from Zoe. "Also, one hand spanning the back of my neck." Elle shivered at the thought.

"While we are on the topic, do you have any other triggers? Smells, maybe?" asked Zoe.

"Not that I can think of."

"You're lucky. Nick absolutely can't chew cinnamon gum and kiss me. I should ask you, Alan. Is there anything that triggers you?"

"Not in the way the two of you are discussing. But I do get annoyed when people don't use the Oxford comma or believe a former vice president invented the internet."

Elle covered her mouth. Zoe laughed. "Elle, be careful with the texts you send. I've noticed you leave punctuation out. You don't want the comma police coming for you."

Alan smiled but didn't join in their laughter.

Zoe conferred with her notes. "Moving on. You will share a stateroom that has a separate bedroom. You have both offered to take the couch. I suggest you each take a week on it."

Elle and Alan nodded in unison.

"I have a note here from Melanie. According to Abbie, Alan is stiff when he holds Elle. She suggests you two practice being in each other's personal space and recommends slow dancing to '80s love ballads like they did at proms in the '80s. From the movies I've seen, you basically hug each other while shuffling in a slow circle. There is a link to an '80s dance remix and several clips of movies with people dancing this way in case Alan needs research first." Zoe covered her mouth, attempting to contain her laughter, then paled and ran from the room.

Alan pushed his chair back. "Wha—"

Elle blocked him at the doorway. "*Mrs.* Gooding ran to the bathroom."

"How do you know? Something could be wrong."

"*Mrs.* Gooding," Elle put even more emphasis on the title hoping he'd take the hint. "Sit back down. If she isn't back in a couple of minutes, I'll go check on her."

"But—"

"Trust me. *Mrs.* Gooding is fine."

Alan's eyes widened. "Oh, she's—"

Elle shook her head. "Client confidentiality. Don't ask, because I can't tell."

"But she isn't our client."

"For the weekend, she is. Her husband's firm contracted us to add a team for the dinner."

"How did I miss that?"

"Maybe because you aren't doing all the scheduling since you are prepping for a big assignment."

Alan sat back down and checked the Hastings app on his tablet. He swiped through page after page. "I feel so out of touch, and I haven't even left yet."

Elle reached for the tablet and turned it facedown on the table. "I think the first thing we need to do is teach you how to disconnect from the office."

Alan circled the perimeter of the empty ballroom. One of the attendees had left her coat. ZoElle's voice came over the comms link. "Found the coat. I'll run it to the car."

Alex's voice answered. "I'll meet you on the stairs."

Returning to the command room, Alan shut down the computer. "Last car has left. I'm sending my comms up with Elle and signing out."

"Good night, Alex." Alan acknowledged his brother's comment. Not until ZoElle entered the room did he realize they were alone in the building. Catering had left hours ago, and the cleaning crew wasn't scheduled for an hour.

"Another quiet event—just the way we like them." ZoElle returned Alex's comms to the case. "Oh, ouch!"

"What?"

"I used one of the old comms tonight, and it's stuck in my hair. Can you help me?" ZoElle turned her back to Alan, the earpiece pinched between her fingers. The wire disappeared into her bun and reappeared for an inch before it threaded down the back of her jacket.

"I think you wrapped the wire up in your bun." Alan pulled out a bobby pin, then another.

ZoElle gasped. "When the waiter ran into me, I caught my hair on a hook on the wall. I put it back up without a mirror. I must have gotten the cord caught then."

As Alan pulled out the last pin and unwound her soft hair, a faint citrus scent tickled his nose. He'd never noticed how her hair smelled. Well, not recently. Last summer, she'd used a berry-scented shampoo. He finger combed the comms cord loose and stepped back. "You're free."

ZoElle dropped the earpiece down the back of her jacket and pulled the unit free. "Thanks. I guess I should make sure I use the wireless ones from now on."

"Probably wise." Alan checked each comm unit to make sure it was turned off before closing the case.

"Do you need to stay until the custodial crew arrives?"

"I should."

"We have an entire ballroom to ourselves. Maybe we should dance." ZoElle's suggestion caught him off guard.

"I figured we could practice at the gym one morning." Really, not at all. There wasn't much point. Relaxing around ZoElle was dangerous.

"The gym? In front of everyone who's working out before going on duty?"

His brothers and the employees watching them from the treadmill and weight bench wouldn't make touching ZoElle any easier. "I hadn't thought of everyone watching."

"I have Abbie's playlist." ZoElle tapped on her phone.

"I don't trust my sister." Or maybe he didn't trust himself, not when he was noticing things about ZoElle, like how she was perfect dance-partner height.

"Fine. You pick the music. We only have a week to literally get our act together."

As much as he wanted to, he couldn't argue her point. Between prepping for their assignment, Adam and September's wedding, and their normal assignments, there wouldn't be much time. Besides, he'd taken social dance in college. He could do more than a two-step shuffle, and the ballroom floor was better for dancing than the sparring mat. Alan stacked the equipment cases by the door. "Let's dance."

He opened his music app and chose five songs. "Do you know how to swing?"

"You mean like the '50s? Of course. My parents taught dance at a Fred Astaire Dance Studio. They may have entered me in a few competitions over the years."

"I didn't know you danced." Alan wondered if his social-dance classes could compete.

"There are probably a lot of things you don't know about me."

Alan started the music and held out his hands. After a few awkward movements, he found the beat and led her through more elaborate steps. Halfway through the song, he froze midspin.

ZoElle tripped to a stop. "What?"

"I realized the rest of the sequence puts you in one of those hugs you said was a trigger."

ZoElle dropped his hand and danced her part of the sequence, stopping midturn. "There? I don't think dancing will bother me because I know the steps and how it spins out. Can we try it?"

Alan restarted the song. At the end, ZoElle smiled. "See, dancing worked fine. I haven't been dancing in a few years."

The next song worked for the foxtrot.

ZoElle came out of a spin laughing. "We should have no problem dancing on the ship. What else do you know?"

"Waltz." Alan had learned more sensual dances during his third semester of dance, but no way was he going to admit that to a woman who had danced her entire childhood.

"Tango? Mamba?"

"I don't remember." Total lie, but the basic steps were nothing like on the TV dance shows.

ZoElle raised her brows. "Hmm. Let's do the dance your sister suggested."

"But these are much more fun."

"True, but Abbie's point was we need to relax with each other. With the waltz and foxtrot, you can get away with not quite touching me and proper posture. I know you aren't happy about this, but you are going to have to touch me. Channel one of your brothers with their girlfriends or wives. Pretend you like me. Or better yet, Preston. Even with the triplets, he is always looking at Abbie like she is the only person in the room."

"Unless one of the boys has a dirty diaper." Alan deflected the main issue. He'd been pretending not to like her for so long, it was a habit. How could he break it without breaking rules and crossing lines?

ZoElle rolled her eyes. "Your playlist or Abbie's. Two songs. If you can't relax, we need to tell Jethro and Melanie we have a problem and this assignment won't work."

A problem he would never live down. Alan opened the playlist Abbie sent and chose a Peter Cetera song. He wrapped his arms around ZoElle's waist, and she put her arms around his neck. They shuffled around the floor.

She laughed softly, her breath tickling his neck. "Breathe. I'm not going to bite you. Pretend I'm your high school prom date."

"I didn't go. I mean I went, but we left after dinner. She got food poisoning or something." Alan later heard his date had shown up at the dance with someone else. A fact ZoElle didn't need to know.

"Fine. Pretend I'm the girl you had a crush on your freshman year of college."

"I didn't have a crush."

"You took social dance. You had a crush."

"I never asked her out." He was the shy brother. Being built like a football player but preferring computers put him at odds with most of the women he met. He didn't have Alex's muscles, Adam's confidence, or Andrew's flair. Pretending ZoElle was someone else felt like a betrayal. Dancing with her was fun, even in the go-no-place shuffle.

The music changed to another song. ZoElle looked into his eyes. "Better. Whatever you are thinking now, hold on to it."

You have beautiful eyes, and you are fun to be with. The song ended, and Alan stepped back. "So, we are good?"

ZoElle nodded. "I'll see you Monday."

Saturday and Sunday had never felt so long.

A DOZEN WEDDING DRESSES HUNG from the tall rack, creating a wall of white in the middle of Abbie's library.

"So many choices." Elle lifted the first wedding dress from its hanger.

"There's more where these came from. We'll find you the perfect dress." Abbie switched the baby in blue to her other hip.

Elle didn't want perfect. The perfect dress would be for a real wedding, which this was not. "You didn't need to bring them here. I could have stopped by Harmon Media."

"Harmon Media's entertainment shows, magazines, and web media are our biggest grossing section. We hire the nosy paparazzi. Paparazzi that would spoil this charade. I took a risk with the photo shoot. No way was I letting the warehouse people know what was happening. Adam and September's wedding is a balancing act, but she is a star who was going to make the news anyway. Believe me, you don't want someone figuring out Alan is getting married too. Two of my brothers getting married the same week would be news." Abbie put the boy in a bouncy chair next to his brothers. "Or worse, not getting married. Given your media presence, having a false story out there wouldn't be a good thing."

"Oh, I didn't think of that." Elle walked into the screened area and changed into the first dress. "Abbie, can you help me with the buttons?"

Abbie had set up a wall of mirrors—nothing as fancy as a bridal shop but more than a normal house would have.

Elle took one look in the mirror and shook her head. "Way too much skin. Alan will not be able to look at me."

Abbie laughed. "Or he won't be able to take his eyes off you."

Elle lifted her hair so Abbie could unbutton her. "I'm not trying to seduce your brother. He's made his opinion of me perfectly clear over the past year. I need something simple and modest."

The next two dresses were definite no's. Elle didn't even bother trying them on. The next dress, a satin ball gown, felt wonderful, but the off-the-shoulder sleeves offered little support. No amount of padding would prevent the bodice from slipping.

"Strapless was out for me too." Abbie helped her out of her dress. "After having the boys, I can do strapless, but I really don't want the entire world looking at my increased cup size. Here, try this one—long sleeves, and the back isn't too low."

The dress felt good, almost too good, as the satin hugged her curves in all the right places. Elle craned her neck to see the back, which stopped above her bra strap. "This one might work. From the front, it covers as much of me as my regular office clothes."

Abbie walked around Elle, viewing the dress from all sides. "I think my brother would approve. The cut flatters your hips too. There are a couple more you should try on."

The next dress had Abbie giggling.

"I look like a mermaid coming out of the surf. I don't think this is a good look for me. "

The last dress took Elle's breath away before Abbie even finished the buttons. The tulle ball-gown skirt with lace overlays and sleeves was the dress she pictured herself walking down the aisle holding her father's arm in. Hints of her skin showed through the lace, enough to feel like a beautiful woman without making the groomsmen drool.

"This is the one, isn't it?" Abbie squeaked and covered her mouth with both hands as she stepped back. "It's a Mateo original. I told him about you and showed him your photo."

Elle turned slowly in front of the mirrors. "It's beautiful. If I were getting married, I wouldn't have to look any further. But this is only pretend. I think the long-sleeved one is better for my imaginary ceremony." She couldn't stop looking in the mirror. Elle traced the lace flower pattern on the three-quarter sleeve and took a final look in the mirror. It wasn't fair, really. Many brides took weeks to find their perfect dress. She'd found hers, but the dress would be out of style long before she ever became a bride.

September and Adam walked back down the aisle, and the minister clapped his hands together. "And then you go live your happily ever after, which you have to work on more than you did this wedding."

Jethro and Melanie exchanged knowing smiles. "Lots more work," said Dad. "Now we have the non-wedding to photograph. Fake bride and groom, hurry. The real rehearsal dinner is waiting."

The photographer from last week's photo shoot slipped in through the back door of the sanctuary. ZoElle and Abbie disappeared from the room, and Alan pulled his tux jacket off the back of the pew he'd left it on earlier. Melanie helped him with his bow tie.

Alan tried to stand still. "I'm not so sure about faking a wedding in the church."

"The minister is fine with it. He said it's no different from when they rented the building out for the day to film a movie. He won't even be here."

Abbie entered the room. She'd changed into her matron-of-honor dress, matching the flowers adorning the room.

Alex tapped Alan on the shoulder. "Here's your boutonniere."

Melanie took the flower from him. "Let me pin it on."

"You know I wouldn't wear a tux two days in a row for just anyone." Alex slapped Alan on the shoulder.

"You know I am *not* getting married, right?" Alan growled at his brother.

The photographer interrupted any answer Alex might have given. "Groom, I need you here." He indicated the spot Adam had occupied during the rehearsal. "Best man and matron of honor, please take your places. You there, open the door."

Jethro Hastings opened the door at the back of the sanctuary to reveal ZoElle standing in the doorway with a small bouquet in hand. Alan missed his next breath. Unlike the suits she normally wore to work, the white dress hugged her figure and sparked his imagination.

"Bride, on my cue, slowly walk down the aisle. I need to take photos." The photographer moved into position. "And slow walk. Smile. Look down at your flowers and up at the groom. Shy smile."

He'd taken a punch to the chest more times than he could count in his life—nasty ones where his brain wondered if his heart could remember to beat and his lungs fill with air. ZoElle's eyes meeting his caused the same reaction, only as if his brothers had double-teamed him.

Alex nudged him. "Breathe, man."

"Good. Good. Eyes on the groom." The photographer stepped to the side, his camera clicking.

Unlike the rehearsal, there wasn't any recorded music. Yet as ZoElle glided toward him, Alan was sure he could hear Pachelbel's Canon. His necktie tightened around his throat. Words to describe the lovely woman walking toward him failed him. It must be the dress. The point of a wedding dress was to make the bride look magnificent. Alan swallowed, glad he wouldn't have to talk during the fake ceremony. He couldn't take his eyes off ZoElle even when the photographer turned to snap his photo.

"Good, good. Groom, take her hand. Yes, just like that. Keep your back to me." Camera flashes burst behind them. ZoElle gazed steadily into his eyes. His heart rate elevated to the same rate as when he sprinted 500 yards.

"Turn to face each other. Groom, put the ring on the bride."

Alan froze. "Ring?"

Abbie stepped around ZoElle. "Sorry, I meant to give the ring to you earlier." She handed him a simple band.

ZoElle held out her hand. Light reflected off the diamond ring on her left hand. Where had it come from?

"Groom? Put the band on the finger."

Struggling to move, he stared at the ring Abbie had given him. This was so wrong.

Alex nudged him. "Come on. I want to get to dinner. It's only a ring. You didn't even take any vows."

Of course not. Unlike Alex's semifake marriage last summer, this was all for the camera. Alan took a deep breath—and dropped the ring.

It rolled under ZoElle's dress.

Giggles and laughter filled the room. Lifting her skirt six inches, ZoElle stepped back, revealing the ring's resting place. Alan dove for it.

"Groom, take five. You're too red. Bride, let's get a photo of the train." The photographer directed Elle to a corner of the room.

"You okay?" Alex tipped his head.

"I need some air." Alan hurried to the exit. The last thing he needed right now was any brotherly advice. Especially from the one who had his fake marriage turn very much real. This wasn't a wedding. No minister or judge was pronouncing anything. But if the wedding wasn't real, why was he so nervous?

"Alan?"

He turned at the sound of his mother's voice. "Yes, Mom?"

"Are you going to go through with this?"

"I've never been a great actor. Putting a ring on someone's hand when she isn't going to be my wife, is—I don't know—weird."

"And it probably doesn't help to have your siblings and their significant others watching."

Alan tried to laugh, but it came out as a strangled cough. "I don't understand why I'm nervous. She looks so different in the wedding dress, not like the ZoElle I know."

"Abbie didn't look like a bodyguard in her wedding dress either."

"That isn't what I mean—I don't know what I mean. Let's go get this over with."

The ring slid on the second time he tried, and the photographer got the photos he wanted.

"Only a few photos left. I don't want to direct you in between shots. First the groom will kiss the bride, and not a little peck like in the studio. I want a robust kiss. One that makes the audience smile and clap but not be embarrassed. Then you are going to look around, smile, and leave the room together smiling because as soon as you get to the car, you can give each other the kiss you wanted to at the altar. Groom, think of getting to the hotel and undoing all those buttons."

An image of undoing the buttons running down the back of ZoElle's dress filled Alan's mind. He pushed the thought away. This was ZoElle he was thinking about. Wrong, wrong, wrong.

"Ready? You may kiss the bride."

Alan placed his hands on either side of ZoElle's waist as he had when they'd danced. As he closed the distance between them, he could have sworn he saw her blush before she closed her eyes. Her lips were soft and cool, which didn't account for the sudden warmth he felt. Alan eased his hand around her back and pulled her closer, keeping the kiss. Was the moan from him or her? There was going be trouble with this assignment that had nothing to do with protecting their client.

The trouble was Alan liked kissing ZoElle.

ELLE CLAPPED ALONG WITH THE others as the bride and groom kissed again.

Harmony tugged on her new father's pant leg. "Me kiss!" She threw her arms up with complete faith that Adam would lift her. The raspberry kiss she gave Adam was met with cheers and laughter. September hugged them both, and the new Mr. and Mrs. Hastings left the reception hall with their daughter.

Elle resumed her place at the coat check. She helped Alex's wife, Kimberly, with her coat. "Nothing like starting a honeymoon with a baby."

Alex came from another room carrying several gift bags. "That's why we haven't gone on ours yet."

Kimberly blushed at his wink. "Hurry, I need to get home to feed Clay." She turned to Elle. "Now that he's sleeping through the night, I hate to get him off his schedule."

"Sleeping through the night. Is that a thing?" asked Abbie as Preston helped her with her coat.

"Yes." Kimberly took the gift bags from Alex as he put his coat on. "Aren't any of your boys sleeping yet?"

Preston hugged his wife from behind. "They all can, but if one wakes up, they all wake up. We got two nights in a row last week without interruption. I woke up because of the silence and couldn't go back to sleep for fear I'd not hear the baby monitor."

"I understand that's the problem with triplets." Kimberly kissed Alex on the cheek and took his arm. "Abbie, call me, and I'll bring Clay over for the afternoon for a cousins date."

Andrew and Jordan entered the coatroom.

"Where have you two been?" asked Abbie.

"Talking." They answered over each other. The youngest Hastings brother reddened as he exchanged a glance with his blushing fiancée. "We were discussing our wedding plans."

"I hope it's a traditional wedding. Mom needs more of those after what Alex and I did." Abbie slipped her arm around Preston's waist. "And Alan is going on a honeymoon before he proposes."

Elle shrunk into the corner as the others laughed, heat rising in her face. It wasn't like it was a real honeymoon or anything. Although, if Alan kissed her too many times like he did last night for the camera, she might have a difficult time convincing her heart. They'd avoided each other at Adam's wedding and reception, which wasn't hard since Alan was part of the wedding party and she wasn't. Although she had hoped for a dance to the live band.

Alan entered, and his siblings started laughing again. He looked from one to another and then at Elle. "I'm not sure what you're laughing about, but since someone embarrassed Elle, I won't ask." He glared at his sister before turning to Elle. "Plans changed. I'll pick you up at 5:45. The pilots want to leave a half hour earlier."

Abbie stopped laughing. "Did you let Adam and September know?"

"Yes. They are going to go get Harmony's things and take her to your house tonight."

"Darling, we better hurry home." Preston nodded at everyone as he led Abbie out of the room.

Alan slapped Andrew on the back. "Thanks for coming back to help cover the teams for a week while Adam's gone."

"No problem. I wanted to see some of the latest tech anyway. Earring communication devices would have so many uses in Hollywood if the principal would agree to wear them."

Jordan wove her hand through Andrew's. "No way, no how, do I want my bodyguard to listen in on my life."

"Even if he's your fiancé?"

"You aren't my bodyguard. And you're what I don't want him to hear." Jordan pulled Andrew into a passionate kiss.

Alan cleared his throat. "Witnesses in the room."

Jordan giggled. "Sorry. Not sorry." She left with Andrew.

"Hey, someone left their coat."

Elle looked around the room. "I don't see one."

Alan pointed.

"That's mine." She took the soft white coat off the hanger.

"Really? I didn't recognize it."

She slid her left arm into the sleeve. "Believe it or not, you don't know everything about me." The right sleeve dangled behind her. She twisted to get it.

Alan stepped back. "Sorry, I didn't mean to offend."

Elle's thumb caught the sleeve, but she still couldn't get her arm in. "Not offended, but could you pretend to be a gentleman for a moment and help me with my coat?" She turned her back to him. Alan was only semihelpful as he seemed determined to slide the coat on without touching her. Finally, the coat rested on her shoulders.

Elle took a deep breath. "I know this will be a difficult two weeks for you. Us. I don't have cooties, and I won't poison you with my touch. This whole thing would go better if you could at least pretend to like me. I promise I'll stay out of your way as much as possible when we are alone. But if you keep treating me like a pariah in private, it's going to make pretending in public much harder. You wouldn't even dance with me tonight. Yet you danced with every other female who works with you. I can't do this if you hate me." Elle turned. Alan was standing much closer to her than she realized.

He lifted his hand almost to her cheek and let it hover. Elle tried to breathe normally under his scrutiny. He leaned forward. Would he kiss her again? Without an audience? Her heartbeat accelerated, not getting the message that a kiss could only be for practice. Not that they needed any practice since last night's kiss.

Say something!

Alan dropped his hand and stepped back. His mouth opened, but no words came out. He spun around and exited the coatroom. Abbie was wrong. The next two weeks would be about as far as one could get from a honeymoon. It was going to be more like a work assignment dreamed up in Hades.

Alan patrolled a corridor lit by a neon-blue light. Every time he turned a corner, he ran into more closed doors. An alarm rang. He looked around for the intruder or a fire, but there was no danger. They turned another corner, searching for the source of the incessant buzzing.

The ping of an alert tone on Alan's phone woke him up. He reached for his phone.

5:34.

How had he missed his alarm? He was supposed to be at ZoElle's in ten minutes.

A second alert sounded. He opened his phone to read the two texts.

The first was from ZoElle.

— **Do you have the communication earrings? I gave them back after the test, but I don't remember seeing them after that.**

The earrings—where were they? On his dresser with the Valentine's Day gift he had never given her. And probably never would. The necklace was much too personal. He hadn't thought it through. He'd return it after the assignment was over.

I'll bring them.

The other text was from Abbie.

— **Bon voyage. Sorry I embarrassed Elle.**

Alan didn't bother replying. He was sure he didn't want to know what she was referring to, even if he had the time. He'd have to shower and shave on the plane. Preston had loaned Adam and September his private jet for their honeymoon. The couple had agreed to drop off his parents, ZoElle, and him in San Diego so they could stay at the reception and make the ship on time.

He was out of the parking lot headed west when he realized he'd forgotten the earrings and did a U-turn. When he finally reached ZoElle's apartment building, she was pacing out front and rubbing her arms to keep warm.

"What's wrong? You're never late." She bit out the question, more accusation than inquiry.

No way was he explaining how he hadn't slept after nearly kissing her last night at Adam's reception. He'd only had one glass of champagne, so he couldn't blame intoxication. Watching his siblings make out all evening was the only reasonable explanation—a simple case of what Mom called "Monkey see, monkey do."

Alan put her suitcases in the back of his SUV. "I overslept."

ZoElle got in the passenger seat and turned up the heater. "I didn't think the Hastings ever overslept. I've been on overnight assignments with all your brothers. They're always the first to be up and checking when there's a bump in the night."

"Yup." Alan pulled out on the street and signaled for a left turn.

"Don't go that way. There's construction, and they've blocked the street off."

He looked at the GPS panel. There was no sign of irregular traffic, so he turned left. ZoElle huffed. Raindrops dotted his windshield. No wonder the pilots wanted to leave early. Alan checked the temperature on his dash. Above freezing. Hopefully that meant no black ice.

Three blocks later, he ran into a detour that held him at a stoplight for two cycles. ZoElle pinched her lips together and looked out the raindrop-pelted window.

"Just say it," he growled.

"Say what?"

"I told you so."

ZoElle glanced in his direction. "I wasn't going to say it."

"But you were thinking it."

"Of course I was. But I am not rude enough to say I told you so."

The light turned green, and Alan took the ramp to the 90. His phone rang, and he answered on the hands-free.

"Where are you?" His mother skipped the niceties.

"About fifteen minutes out."

"What?" Melanie's voice was raised.

"I slept in." The admission stung.

"Oh. Is Elle with you?"

"I'm here, Mrs. Hastings," answered ZoElle.

"It's Melanie, dear." His mother's voice lost the hard edge she'd used with him. "Come directly to the hangar. We're ready to depart."

"Will do." Alan shut off the phone. Great. Now his parents were upset with him.

Thirteen minutes later, he parked behind Preston's private hangar. ZoElle jumped out and retrieved her bags from the back. Alan hurried after her. The plane was already on the tarmac.

Adam waved from the doorway. "Bring your bags to the main cabin. They already closed the cargo hold."

ZoElle beat Alan to the stairs. Adam met her at the bottom, grabbed her large suitcase, and they disappeared into the belly of the plane. Alan's duffel caught on the railing as he ran up the stairs. He tugged on it, but instead of breaking free, it ripped, its contents dumping onto the wet tarmac. Biting back an expletive, Alan tossed his computer bag into the plane and rushed to gather his items as the rain soaked them.

Adam ran to help him. ZoElle rushed down the stairs with a large black garbage bag she held open as Adam and Alan raced to pick up the clothing, tossing items from where they stood. Adam tossed a pair of boxers, overshooting the bag. They hit ZoElle's shoulder and bounced in.

"Careful." Alan gathered up the rest of his underwear. He'd never intended for her to know the answer to "Boxers or briefs?" during this job.

"I think we got it all." ZoElle closed the bag and hurried into the plane, Adam following. A toothbrush sat in a puddle near the wheel. Alan ignored it. He could get one aboard the ship.

Someone handed him a towel.

Jethro pointed Alan to the back of the plane. "Put those things in the drawers under the bed. You can repack after takeoff."

Alan passed ZoElle. Her hair was wrapped in a towel. Why hadn't she been wearing a coat? Chicago in February demanded one, even en route to a tropical vacation. He waited while Adam put an armful of items in a drawer. "Bro, you look like you were up all night. Maybe you got this wrong. I'm the one on the real honeymoon."

"Back off." Alan slammed the drawer and went to take a seat across the aisle from ZoElle.

Before he got his seat belt fastened, the plane started to taxi. He pulled out his phone and listed the problems he needed to solve.

1. New toothbrush
2. Suitcase
3. Dry clothes
4. Shower and shave

ZoElle reached across the aisle and tapped his arm. "I have a collapsible in my suitcase if you need it."

"A collapsible?"

"Suitcase. You know the thing you put in your suitcase so when you buy souvenirs—an extra suitcase to take them home in?"

"Souvenirs are a waste of money. Besides, this isn't a vacation."

"I noticed. If you grumble much more, I'll file for a divorce before we land. Take a deep breath. We have four hours of flight time. It will work out."

"Really? You aren't the one without dry clothes."

"When I flew out to California with Kimberly last year, there was a blow dryer in the plane's bathroom. You won't be able to dry everything, but you only need one set of clothes to get on the ship."

Everything about this was wrong—his clothes, his timing, and ZoElle trying to solve his problems. "Then I'll still have wet clothes."

"Yes, and we are in a luxury stateroom complete with valet service. They will be more than happy to help the unfortunate groom who has nothing to wear."

Two rows in front of him, Adam chuckled. Alan ignored it. He didn't need any more ribbing over his fake-groom status.

Sometime during their conversation, the plane reached cruising altitude. Alan unbuckled his seat belt and headed for the bathroom. ZoElle followed him.

He stopped at the doorway to the bedroom. "Where are you going?"

"I thought I would work on drying your clothes while you showered."

"No."

ZoElle took a small step back. "I'm only trying to help."

"I don't need your help."

The color drained from her face. Alan knew he should apologize, but no way was she going to touch his soggy underwear.

Jethro tapped ZoElle on the shoulder. "You enjoy the flight. I'll help my son."

Alan dug through the drawers, looking for his shaving kit.

His father sat down on the bed. "I've been patient for several days as I have watched you treat Elle with coldness and disrespect. I don't know what happened between you two, but your mother and I taught you to respect others, especially women. What you did is no way to treat your wife, pretend or not."

Having found his shave kit and a dry pair of sweatpants, Alan slammed the drawer shut. "ZoElle isn't my wife."

"She is for the next fifteen days. Give me some of your things, and I'll dry them while you shower and get your head on straight."

The heat of his father's glare filled Alan until the shame of his actions burned. He longed to explain his reaction to ZoElle's kiss and ask for advice on maintaining their friendship, but the question was too embarrassing, and so he headed for the shower.

THE LINE TO BOARD THE ship snaked around the terminal. Melanie nodded toward a sign indicating first-class passengers, where the line was shorter. "You two get the short line, while the old folks get the long one."

"Doesn't seem fair after forty-five years, does it, hon?" The cheap toupee covering Jethro's bald head bounced as he nodded. Elle suppressed a smile at her boss's new look.

Melanie patted her own grayed hair. "Let's leave the newlyweds alone, dear. I'm sure we'll see them later."

Elle followed Alan into the other line void of the buffer Jethro and Melanie had provided since his eruption on the plane. In a few minutes, they would leave their bags, and their hands would be free. Ahead of them in the security line she recognized Cassie Evans-Johnson from the photos Jethro had shown her. Cassie and her new husband had two bodyguards with them.

"Ticket? Passport?" The uniformed attendant held out her hand. Alan handed his over first. "Oh, our other newlyweds. Welcome."

Elle handed her passport and ticket over for inspection.

"Mrs. Hastings."

Elle looked behind her, expecting to see Melanie. The attendant laughed. "Not accustomed to the name yet?"

"No, I'm not." She smiled at the attendant and then Alan, hoping she looked besotted.

"Most brides don't have the chance to change their documents. Would you like the crew to address you as Mrs. Hastings?"

"Yes, by the end of our trip, I'll be used to the name." Elle took her documents back.

Alan waited and took her bags from her, setting them on the conveyor belt to be screened. Another attendant sent her through the metal detector. Alan followed. As soon as they cleared the area, Alan took her by the hand, weaving their fingers together. At last he'd gone into acting mode. Elle ignored the sensations her traitorous body created in response to his touch.

"Mr. and Mrs. Hastings, welcome. I'm Jennifer. I will be one of your personal valets on the cruise. May I show you to your stateroom?"

Elle smiled up at Alan, surprised to find him smiling back, though his eyes were still troubled.

"Yes, please," answered Alan.

Jennifer pointed out several amenities along the way, including the lounge and pool for only the premiere staterooms, told them of the valet service they could ring for, and reminded them of their mandatory safe-ship drill before departure. "It's embarrassing for us as well as the newlyweds if we have to track you down in your room."

Elle couldn't help blushing at the insinuation.

Alan rubbed his thumb along her knuckles. "Don't worry. We'll be there."

Jennifer stopped at the door and handed Alan the key cards. "These doors swing shut on their own. Would you like me to hold them while you carry your bride across the threshold?"

Before the word *no* crossed Elle's lips, Alan scooped her into his arms. She flung her arm around his neck for balance.

"Is there anything you need before I leave you?"

Elle held on to Alan's neck since he hadn't put her down. "Yes, my husband was being gallant this morning in the rain, and his suitcase broke. His clothes are sopping wet. Can we get them laundered?"

"Ring for me as soon as your bags arrive." Jennifer shut the door behind her.

Alan set her in the center of the combination dining-seating area.

Elle stepped away. "My goodness, I could tell this room was over-the-top just from the ship's diagram, but it's three times the size, or more, of the stateroom I stayed in on my last cruise. And it isn't even the biggest." She opened the door to their private balcony and walked to the railing. A blonde leaned over the rail on the other side of the privacy wall.

Elle waved.

"Hello. Are you on a honeymoon too?" Cassie Evans's accent would have given her away as a Texan if Elle hadn't already known.

"Yes. I'm Elle."

"Cassie. We must chat sometime." Cassie waved and disappeared.

Elle walked back into the suite. Alan sat on the couch typing furiously into his phone.

"I made first contact with Cassie."

"Mm-hmm." He didn't look up.

Elle explored the rest of the suite. Folding doors separated the bedroom from the living room. A welcome basket sat on the bed with a pair of champagne glasses nestled next to two bottles of champagne. Neither of them drank on duty. Elle didn't drink off duty either and suspected Alan didn't often. A closer look proved the bottles were not true champagne at all but the nonalcoholic cider.

Elle turned over the card. "Bon voyage. Love, Abbie." That explained the copious amounts of chocolate and the bottle of ibuprofen. There was a sci-fi book, two romance novels, and two decks of cards hidden under his-and-her photo frames. Elle put everything back and took a photo. She'd almost forgotten the need to capture the honeymoon in photos. She'd avoided looking at the photos of their wedding loaded onto her phone.

After inspecting the large bathroom, Elle found Alan still sitting on the couch.

"Selfie time."

"What?" His eyes didn't leave his phone.

"We need to explore the ship and take selfies."

"As soon as I finish this."

Elle looked over his shoulder. He was logged into the Hastings app. "Are you doing Alex's job?"

"I'm doing my job."

"Which has been assigned to Alex for the next two weeks. He can handle scheduling and planning without your interference."

Alan finally looked up from his screen. "What did you want me to do?"

"Come take a selfie on the balcony, and then we can go explore the ship like normal passengers."

"We need to meet Cassie and her husband." Alan followed her out to the deck.

"Didn't you hear me say I made first contact?" Elle kept her voice low in case someone was on the other side of the privacy wall. She leaned her back against the railing and held up her phone.

Alan joined her, standing stiffly by her side.

"Can you smile?" *And pretend to like me?*

Alan put his arm around her and leaned in. Elle snapped the photo. "Kiss me on the forehead." Alan pressed his lips to her temple. He'd have to do better than that in public.

"Look at the camera." Elle stood on her toes and kissed his cheek, still smooth from the shave on the airplane. His scent mingled with the salty ocean air, a pleasant combination. She snapped the last selfie. "Shall we go explore?"

"My clothes aren't here yet."

"They probably won't be for another hour. Adam's shirt looks great on you." The polo was slightly loose in the shoulders, the light-blue complementing his eyes. September was right. She should write ballads about the Hastings brothers' blue eyes.

Elle turned away before she thought too deeply about them.

Alan took her hand. "I'm sorry for yelling at you on the plane."

Elle turned but kept her focus on the line where the ocean met the sky. "It's okay. You had a nasty morning."

"No, it's not okay. We used to be friends, but I've been a jerk lately."

"Your dad told you to apologize, didn't he?" She hadn't missed the pointed looks Jethro and Melanie had given him since he'd emerged from the bedroom on the plane shortly before landing.

"Yes, but—"

Elle held up her hand. "We're good. Let's go to work."

"ZoElle—"

This time she looked him in the eye. "Don't call me ZoElle. I go by Elle." Years of school bullies had removed the Zo from her name as zoo comparisons grew old.

For a moment, she thought he'd argue.

Still holding her hand, he led her out the door. "Let's go explore."

They didn't see their principals, Cassie and Dr. Johnson, until the safety meeting, when they were on the opposite side of the room. Unsurprisingly, his parents were in their evacuation group, as were the bodyguards he'd seen earlier. Both stood several paces away.

Alan recognized the taller one from the time he'd helped Abbie when she was undercover and in trouble a couple of years ago. He couldn't recall the name and longed to pull out his phone and check his records. However, Abbie had lectured him several times about not looking at his phone in public while undercover.

A crew member welcomed them aboard and started the safety instructions. Alan surveyed the crowd. Cassie's husband stood behind her, arms wrapped around her waist. He whispered in her ear, and Cassie blushed.

Alan looked at where his hand met ZoElle's. Compared to other couples in the group, they barely looked like they were together. Compared to his brothers and brother-in-law, he looked like he was not even dating. Keeping his fingers intertwined with ZoElle's, he lifted their arms over her head and stepped behind her. She let out a soft gasp, then settled to the new position, leaning back on his chest and rubbing the back of his hand with her free one. His free hand rested on her waist. This wasn't a position they'd practiced or approved, but it was similar to their dance moves.

Another crew member demonstrated how to use the life jackets. Alan tried to focus on the lecture, but ZoElle's fingers tracing designs on the back of his hand kept distracting him. Her hair was soft against his cheek.

When the lecture ended, ZoElle spun out of his hold. Cassie walked over to them. "Elle?"

"Oh, hi, Cassie."

"This is my husband, Case Johnson. And I know, Cassie and Case are only two letters off, but the *a*'s have different sounds." She kissed her husband on the cheek.

"This is Alan, my husband. Sounds so weird to say husband, doesn't it?"

Alan shook Case's hand. The women continued their conversation.

"I know. We got married just yesterday. Every time someone says Mrs. Johnson, I think of my third-grade teacher."

"I look around for my mother-in-law." ZoElle laughed along with Cassie.

"I should have expected this." Case's smile grew wide. "My wife is on board for two hours and makes an entourage of friends."

"That many?"

"We met two other couples celebrating their anniversaries. I think Cassie is already planning our fortieth—not that I mind."

Cassie's eyes narrowed as she studied Alan. "You remind me of someone. What is your last name?"

"Hastings."

"Oh, I know." Cassie pulled out her phone and tapped the screen. "You look like the guy who married September Platt. You know, the Christian singer? They got married yesterday too. It was all over my news feed. I was wor—" She clamped her mouth shut, her face clouding for a moment. "Here, you look just like him. Isn't this you next to him?"

The photo of Alan standing at Adam's side filled Cassie's phone screen.

ZoElle leaned into Alan's shoulder to look. "That's Alan's brother."

"You got married the same day as your brother?"

"Crazy, isn't it? A couple of weeks ago we decided we didn't want to wait. The entire family would be in town, so after Adam and September's wedding, we took advantage of the decorated church and took our vows." ZoElle recited their cover story. "Their sister is the sweetest and helped me find a dress. I can't believe we pulled it off in only a few days. September was great about it. I didn't wear my dress to the reception or anything. I didn't want to steal their day."

"How did you get on this cruise?" asked Case, suspicion tinging his voice.

"My sister, Abbie, has amazing resources. She gave us our honeymoon as a gift." Alan delivered his part of the cover story.

"Hastings…Hastings…Oh, you are that security firm out of Chicago, aren't you? Your sister married Preston Harmon." Cassie laid her hand on ZoElle's arm. "My guilty pleasure is gossip magazines. I work in hospitals and see them all the time." Cassie gasped and covered her mouth. "No way! That is so romantic. You married the bodyguard who rescued you, right? But your name isn't Elle. It's Zoe or something."

ZoElle's hand trembled on Alan's arm. "I'm Elle to my friends."

Alan pulled ZoElle closer. "I'm lucky to be the man who found her."

Case's brow wrinkled. "I assume yours isn't a working honeymoon?"

Alan kissed the top of ZoElle's head. "No way. I only have one priority over the next two weeks."

"So do I. We'll see you around." Case waved and ushered Cassie away.

ZoElle relaxed and took a step away. "Do you think he guessed?"

"Maybe. Are you okay?" As near as he could tell, ZoElle hadn't noticeably reacted to being recognized. Fame from a #MeToo incident wasn't a pleasant thing. Over the last year and a half, he'd watched her smile in public and withdraw as soon as she could. The explanation that she kept speaking out so others wouldn't suffer was noble, but he suspected the toll on her was more than she admitted.

"I didn't think she'd make the connection so fast. Shall we find something to eat? I'm starving."

ZoElle had lied. He knew it as clearly as if it were written across his computer screen. The interaction had bothered her.

"You're sure it's not seasickness?" asked Elle.

Alan's face had paled by degrees ever since dinner. "I told you I'm fine."

Elle sighed. There was no one more difficult to reason with than a man who couldn't admit when things were bad. The ship had only been moving for five hours. Tomorrow they would spend the entire day at sea. If it was seasickness, by dinnertime tomorrow, he'd give in. Elle turned her focus to the stage. The cooking demonstration wasn't exceptionally interesting, but Cassie and Case sat three rows in front of them. Cassie leaned forward in her seat, clearly interested in what the ships' chef was preparing. Case drew random designs on her back. No one else in the room paid the newlyweds any particular attention.

Alan moaned. The dim theater lighting reflected off his sweaty forehead. He wiped it dry with the back of his hand.

One row back and across the aisle, Jethro's yellow Hawaiian shirt stood out like a beacon. Elle opened the Hastings app on her phone and sent Melanie a message. The answer came back quickly.

— **He always gets motion sickness.**

Elle slipped her phone into her purse and took Alan by the elbow. "Come on. You need some air."

He nodded toward Cassie and Case. Elle looked over Alan's shoulder. "Mom." Alan nodded and stepped out into the aisle. Elle followed the signs to the nearest deck and tried not to be obvious about pulling a two-hundred-pound man behind her. The ocean breeze instantly cooled Elle's skin. Alan leaned on the rail, eyes closed, taking deep breaths.

Ten minutes later, he opened his eyes.

"Feeling better?"

"A little."

"Are you wearing a seasickness patch?"

"Didn't think I needed one."

"Did you even get a prescription?" It was one of the items at the top of the packing lists Melanie had given them.

"No."

Elle couldn't stop from rolling her eyes. "I brought extra over-the-counter stuff. Let's go see if it works."

"We are on duty."

"Not anymore. Your parents are."

"But the drugs will make me sleepy."

"Good thing it's night, then."

Alan opened his mouth, then clamped it shut. What little color he had drained away.

Elle pulled a half-gallon zip-top bag out of her purse and held it open in front of Alan. "Use this."

He reached for the bag a second too late.

The acidic smell of vomit hit Elle as hard as the liquid mess coated her from the neck down. The slimy yellow ooze covered her hair, shirt, skirt, and sandals. Passengers on the deck turned in Elle's direction, looks of horror on their faces.

A group of four women wearing coordinating hot-pink, rhinestone-studded shirts proclaiming them to be "Sassy Seniors" rushed over. One pulled an economy-sized package of baby wipes from her over-sized purse. Another hurried across the deck to the pool and grabbed several towels. The tallest steered Alan farther down the railing.

Elle accepted the handful of wipes and started with her hair, then worked on what had dripped into the neckline of her shirt.

"Oh, you poor dear."

"Look at her ring, Pat. I bet they are newlyweds."

"On the bright side, you will always have the best fight come-back. 'Remember the time you used me as a barf bag…?' It will work for years. Right, Georgia?"

The shortest woman handed Elle a towel. "Definitely. Wrap this around your hair like a turban."

Although her hair was still coated, having it contained in the twists of the towel helped lessen the stench. Elle used another towel to wipe as much as she could off her clothing and legs. Three uniformed crew members appeared with more towels and a cleaning kit. One of the women said something, and one of the crew members hurried off, returning with a white robe that had the ship's logo on it.

Georgia turned to the onlookers and waved them away. "Show's over, folks."

Pat and the other woman held up towels. "We'll screen you if you want to take off your shirt before you put on the robe. Here's a plastic bag."

Elle faced out to sea, shucked her shirt, then stuffed it in the bag. Another towel removed most of what had seeped under her top. Once she had the robe wrapped around her, she felt human again. "Where's Alan?"

"Linda and a crew member are taking him down to the sick bay," said Pat. "Step on that towel to get the stuff off your sandals, and we'll take you back to your room."

"We've been on this ship before, so we know how to get there without going through any major areas." Georgia handed the soiled towels to a crew member.

"We should introduce ourselves. I'm Annie, this is Pat, and this is Georgia. You probably didn't see Linda. Don't worry about your man. Linda has four grown boys, and she knows how to handle them."

"I'm Elle. Thank you for your quick thinking."

"Where's your room?" asked Georgia. Elle answered and was whisked away by her escorts.

The three women kept up a conversation mostly made up of tips on how to make her man smile and keep a happy marriage the entire way. Elle allowed the advice to flow over her. Fourteen more days. And if today's disasters were any indication of the future, none of the women's tips would help.

Elle rinsed out her skirt. Whoever did the laundry didn't need to experience the full extent of the damage—although the towels were worse and this probably wasn't the first time the employees had to deal with the effects of seasickness.

Someone banged on the cabin door. Elle giggled at the sight that met her through the peephole. A groggy-looking Adam swayed next to the last of the Sassy Seniors, Linda, who held him up.

As Elle opened the door, she bit back a laugh.

"Here he is, all safe and sound. The doctor gave him a shot. She warned him it might make him sleepy." Linda steered Alan into the suite. "I guess this proves the bigger they are, the harder they fall."

Elle slipped under his arm to relieve Linda of the burden. "I've got him."

Linda set a box on the shelf near the door. "The doctor prescribed seasickness patches for him. She said to let him sleep through the night. I know it's your honeymoon, but may I suggest you sleep on the couch?" A blush showed through the older woman's makeup, making her true meaning clear. "Also, put a wastebasket by the bed."

"I think that's wise."

Linda closed the door behind her. The slurred thank-you crossed Alan's lips a moment too late.

Supporting a man while walking him across the room was more difficult than flipping him on the sparring mat, especially when squeezing through a doorway.

"No, I'll s-sleep on the couch." Alan tried to pull her in the other direction.

Elle stood her ground and got Alan to the side of the king-sized bed. A light push in the center of his chest was all it took to get him to sit.

"You're beautiful. Did I ever tell you that?"

"And you are delirious." Elle grabbed the gift basket from the center of the bed. "Can you take off your shirt? I need to rinse it out."

Alan stripped off the polo. It wasn't the first time Elle had seen his chest, but being this close to him caused her to suck in a breath. "Do you want a clean shirt? Your laundry is back."

"If you are trying to seduce me, that isn't very good." Alan's glassy-eyed grin wasn't very seductive.

"I'm trying to get you into bed so you can sleep. Alone."

"But you asked me to take off my shirt." Alan wrapped an arm around her waist.

Elle extracted herself from his grip. "Can you stand for a minute while I pull the covers back?"

He swayed a little but stayed upright as Elle prepared the bed. "Okay. You can get in bed now."

Alan sat on the edge of the bed and reached for his shoes. He stopped halfway. "The room is spinning."

"I'll get your shoes." Elle knelt in front of him and untied his tennis shoes.

Alan pulled the towel covering her clean hair off her head and ran his fingers through her wet locks. "I noticed your hair first. So pretty."

Elle extricated his hands from her hair and finished removing his shoes and socks. If he wanted his belt and pants off, he'd have to do it. When she stood, he caught her around the waist with both hands.

"I can't forget about the kiss. Can you?" If his eyes were focused, his lopsided grin would lead to another kiss. Fortunately, woozy Alan was easy to resist.

"Alan, I am not having this conversation when you are clearly hallucinating." More like never in a million years talking about any of their kisses. "You need to forget the kiss."

"That is why I was such a jerk today. I was up all night, thinking about you." He rubbed a hand up and down her arm.

Elle pushed him away, and he fell back on the bed, bringing her with him.

Sweet brownie bites! She lay on his chest, her face only inches away from his. A dozen ways to extract herself ran through her mind, but all of them would hurt Alan. She placed both hands on his chest and pushed herself away. Alan rolled over, keeping her in his grasp and pinning her beneath him.

Memories of another person and a different time broke the dam Elle had built to keep her demons at bay. Her breath came out in short gasps. Alan lowered his head, their lips almost meeting.

"No, please, no." She pushed against him and kicked. The training Deidre gave her took over, and her palm connected with his jaw, snapping his head back and rolling him away and onto the floor, where he landed with a thump.

Elle covered her mouth. What had she done?

THE LIGHT FROM THE WINDOW burned Alan's eyes. His jaw felt as if he lost a sparring match with two of his brothers. To celebrate his twenty-first birthday, Alan's friends had taken him on a pub crawl. The result was his first and last hangover—until now. And his head pounded. Fuzzy memories floated around the pain: ZoElle covered with vomit. A woman helping him. A doctor with a syringe. That explained why the sitting part of his anatomy hurt. And sweet ZoElle helping him into bed. He wanted a kiss and...

Clamping both hands on his head, Alan tried to erase the picture of her frightened face. No. Surely that was the remains of some drug-induced nightmare. Rolling out of bed, he found he was shirtless and in yesterday's pants. His chest tightened. Where was ZoElle? He grabbed a shirt off the pile of folded clothes on the dresser and yanked it over his head. The sitting room was empty. Alan checked his watch. She could be at breakfast.

A shadow moved on the balcony. ZoElle sat in one of the deck lounges wrapped in a thin blanket, her knees tucked under her chin—the same position she was in the first time he saw her through the window of her kitchen door, sitting on the floor, tears streaming down her face.

Her face was calm now, her body relaxed, as she stared out over the ocean. ZoElle and everyone else had told him she'd changed in the last year and a half. Maybe she had, or maybe she'd sat there so long the tension had drained from her.

Alan slid the door open. ZoElle turned and gave him a half smile, then looked back to the ocean. "They say there are whales out there."

Alan sat down on the other deck lounge, immediately wishing he had his sunglasses. "Have you seen any yet?"

"No. How are you feeling?"

"Like I have a hangover. Did I hurt you last night?"

She looked at him for a long moment before answering. "No, you didn't hurt me. But from the looks of that bruise on your jaw, I hurt you."

"Will you tell me what happened? I have a memory of your face. You were terrified, and I think I scared you."

"What do you remember?" ZoElle unfolded herself and set her feet on the deck.

"Losing my dinner. A lady in a bright-pink shirt helping me. A shot. And I definitely remember the glitter shirts everywhere. Coming back, and you trying to help me." Alan paused, debating what to say next. "I wanted to kiss you. I didn't take advantage of you, did I?"

"You didn't kiss me."

Alan touched his jaw. "Please, what did I do to deserve this?"

"You didn't deserve it. I overreacted. Deidre taught me too well."

"I frightened you?"

ZoElle watched the ocean. "It wasn't you. It was the old memories. I forgot where I was and who I was with."

Alan didn't ask what memories. ZoElle's rape and the resulting media storm were still garnering attention on rating-seeking talk shows. "I'm sorry I frightened you. You know I wouldn't hurt you."

"I know. And I don't think you would have last night. I think you only wanted a kiss."

Alan searched the horizon looking for answers more elusive than the whales. "But even that was overstepping our boundaries."

"You weren't exactly lucid." A smile softened ZoElle's face.

"It's not an excuse." Nothing was an excuse for trying to force her or anyone to kiss him.

"Considering the day you had yesterday, it's a good one."

He swung around in his chair so he faced Elle. The loungers were too far apart for him to take her hand. "I'm sorry."

"There is nothing to apologize for." Her grin grew wide. "Except throwing up on me. The ladies who helped us reassured me I could get years of apologies out of this blunder. But considering what I did to your jaw and head, I think we are more than even. I'm really sorry I hurt you."

"I deserved it." He rubbed the back of his neck instead of his jaw. No point in making her feel worse for something that was his fault.

"I put your seasickness patches on the bathroom counter."

Being alone with her wasn't helping him to deal with the awkwardness. "I'll go clean up and then we can go to breakfast."

"Sounds good."

Alan stood in the shower, wishing the water could wash the last twenty-four hours away. No more messing up, no more letting his heart lead his head around, and no more hurting ZoElle.

Jethro and Melanie sat across the dining table from Elle and Alan. Someone had arranged for Cassie and Case to be at the table too. Two other groups completed their dinner group. Everyone introduced themselves, Elle accepting congratulations from the two couples from Missouri.

Melanie was the last to introduce their couple. "Jeff and Mel from Illinois. We are celebrating our forty-fifth wedding anniversary. I guess that makes two sets of newlyweds and one set of nearly deads."

One of the women from Missouri coughed into her napkin.

Cassie patted Melanie's arm. "You look years away from nearly dead."

"Thank you, sweetheart. When did you get married?"

"On Valentine's Day. We haven't even been married forty hours," answered Cassie.

"What about you?" Melanie directed her question to Alan.

"We got married on Valentine's Day too."

One of the Missouri women entered the conversation. "That is the sweetest. Tim and I were married fifteen years ago on Valentine's Day. It's the best day to get married."

A waiter came to take their orders.

"Do you have photos of your wedding dresses?" asked Melanie. "You must have looked divine."

Cassie opened her phone and passed it around the table. "We had a small family wedding. Case only has one uncle living, so we kept the celebration small."

"What about you?" asked the woman next to Elle.

Elle opened her phone to the carefully orchestrated wedding photos. "We kind of eloped. Alan's brother got married, and we took advantage of the chapel being decorated and had a short ceremony with family afterward."

"Your dress is amazing. These men must be your brothers-in-law. All those tall, blue-eyed men and muscles. Those must be some genes."

Unbidden, Elle glanced at Jethro. Melanie must have given him brown contacts to match his toupee, which sat better than it had yesterday when they'd boarded. "The eyes are the best. The muscles are a bonus."

Elle's camera finished moving around the table as the entrée was served.

As they ate, Case and Alan discussed which excursions their wives didn't want them going on. Did they even have bungee jumping over a canyon? Elle hadn't noticed the activity in the brochures. The Missouri couples talked among themselves. Cassie talked rapidly to Melanie, leaving Elle and Jethro exchanging a shrug across the table.

One of the Missouri husbands leaned forward. "Did you guys hear about the guy who got sick all over his wife last night?"

"Dear, that isn't a dinner-table topic." His wife's stage whisper carried across the table and farther.

"I heard they were newlyweds. It wasn't either of you two, was it?" asked the other husband.

Case shook his head and laughed. Alan turned as red as the raspberry sauce on the cheesecake in front of him. Jethro raised a brow.

Elle placed a hand on Alan's bicep. "I'm sure whatever you heard was exaggerated. It wasn't that bad."

"We heard they had to bring you a robe to wear back to your room."

Elle smiled. This too would pass.

Alan put his arm on the back of her chair. "I'm lucky she forgave me."

"Rotten way to start the honeymoon. Did the ship's doctor give you a shot of promethazine?" asked Case.

"I'm not sure what it was, but it made me dizzy, and I fell into the wall." He'd used the explanation all day for the bruise on his jaw.

Case slapped Alan on the back and roared with laughter. "Y'all missed the first night of your honeymoon, didn't ya?"

Elle didn't need to check her reflection to know she was redder than Alan, a color that, under normal circumstances, would be almost humanly impossible to achieve. The other couples around the table laughed, including Jethro and Melanie.

The lady next to Elle gave her a side hug. "Don't fret. Jeff had pneumonia on our honeymoon, and I still had a baby nine months later."

Elle smiled and prayed for a change of subject.

The laughter subsided, and the couples went their separate ways. Cassie and Case headed to the ship's casino. Jethro indicated they would follow.

Elle was relieved for the break. She and Alan had shadowed the other couple from a distance most of the day. She'd reached the point where if she had to watch Case push the limits of PDA or play another round of mini golf, she might scream. The mini golf course allowed them an overlook of the main pool area. By the end of the cruise, she should be able to get a hole in one on every obstacle. At one point, a crew member reminded Case and Cassie that they had a private balcony and an in-room hot tub, and the couple disappeared long enough for Elle and Alan to eat lunch.

Alan dropped Elle's hand and opened the door to their suite. "My parents will quiz us tomorrow at our meeting in Cabo."

"It won't be as bad as dinner. Your dad will be concerned about whether you can do your job if you're still sick." Elle sat down on the far end of the couch.

"Only of mini golf. You'd think they'd find something better to do than sit by the pool or in the hot tub for hours." Alan leaned back against the far wall. Every time they'd been alone since their conversation earlier that morning, he'd stayed at least six feet away. The polite distance was probably best, as was talking only about work.

"We need to check with Cassie's security to see if they have a good camera on the pool. If they do, we won't have to be there for hours at a time. The only threat I've wondered about is the man in the Captain America swim trunks."

Alan's face fell into full bodyguard mode. "The one who hit on you?"

"Me and every other blonde on the deck. My gut says he's more desperate than harmful. I don't think he meant anything by it, but it's another reason it would be nice to do the daytime monitoring from behind a camera."

"I still want to see the security control room for this place."

"Do you think they'll let you?"

"Maybe. The sheer number of cameras is mind-boggling. Twenty decks, fifteen accessible to the four thousand passengers, and 1,700 crew members. The casinos alone must have a hundred cameras between them."

"In other words, a computer-security geek's paradise."

He didn't react to her teasing. "Pretty much. Do you want to go work out?"

"No. I'm going to curl up on a deck chair and read a book your sister gave me."

"You can have the bed tonight."

Elle frowned. "The couch will be too short for you. I was fine last night."

"We agreed we would take turns." Alan folded his arms.

"That was before we saw the length of the couch. Since we can't pull out the sleeper-sofa down without housekeeping noticing, I win. I'll take the couch, you get the bed." Elle crossed her arms and tapped her foot.

"I've slept on worse."

"So have I."

The stare down ended when Alan turned away. "I'll be back in an hour."

He left without his workout clothes.

Elle took the book out to the deck but couldn't read. How could she break through this new awkwardness?

THE NEXT MORNING, ALAN EXITED the bathroom to find ZoElle ripping apart the bed he'd slept in and made. Last night, when he'd found her sleeping on the couch, he'd been tempted to carry her to the bed and trade places. But the thought that she might wake up and not realize his intentions and freak out had stopped him. Never, ever, did he want to cause her fear again.

"I just made the bed." He pulled a pair of socks out of his drawer.

"I know, but we have housekeeping to make the beds." She dropped a handful of red lace on the bed and partially covered it with a sheet.

"What is that?"

"Lingerie."

"What?"

"Housekeeping will expect newlyweds to leave the room in a certain state." ZoElle stood back and surveyed her work. "I need the shirt you wore yesterday."

He didn't ask this time, trying hard to not think about what she was doing. He dug his shirt out of the drawer he used for his soiled clothes. His curiosity had him following ZoElle into the sitting room. The sundress she'd worn to dinner lay in a pool a few feet from the door. She stood near the dress and tossed the shirt over her shoulder. It caught on one of the chairs at the table. "Perfect. We have an hour before we dock in Cabo. Our neighbors had room service this morning. Shall we go get breakfast?"

Alan stepped over the dress on his way out the door, his imagination filling in the scene just as housekeeping would. Two weeks of visualizing rated-R bedrooms was...No guy could keep his imagination at bay, especially when he wanted to kiss his partner.

Hours later, as they wandered around the stalls in Cabo's marketplace, Alan monitored the trajectory of his father's ridiculous pink-flamingo shirt. Where had his mother found Dad's wardrobe, and what had she paid him to wear it? His parents entered a small café.

ZoElle haggled with a vendor over the price of a shirt. Her Spanish was better than he expected. When she finished, they entered the café. His parents weren't there.

"You need pink flamingo?" asked a waitress.

"Si."

She pointed to a door at the back of the room. "Private room."

"Gracias." Alan let go of ZoElle's hand as they sidestepped the small tables.

The dining room was not much larger than a broom closet. Its best feature was the privacy, not the ventilation.

Jethro leaned back in his chair. "I ordered us a couple combo dinners."

"Before we start, how are you doing with the seasickness?" Mom's concerned look permeated the extra makeup she wore.

Alan held out ZoElle's chair before he sat down. "The patch seems to work well."

"How bad was it? I've heard several versions of your misadventure."

Jethro's eyes twinkled. "I heard the eruption was comparable to Mount Vesuvius."

ZoElle bit back a laugh.

"Not that bad." Alan glared at his father.

"Speak for yourself. You weren't on the receiving end. The laundry service got the smell and stains out of my clothes, but I had to wash my hair three times."

His parents didn't hold back their laughter.

"That may be one of the worst honeymoon stories I've ever heard." Melanie smoothed Jethro's toupee. "The sad thing is, you can't ever tell the tale in context. I met those four ladies at the bridge tournament. Their version of helping you is horrifying."

"I'm still trying to see the humor in it." Alan forced a smile.

The waitress tapped on the door before entering with their food and bottles of seltzer water.

Jethro prayed over the food before dividing the platters. "I spoke with Peter and Zane. They are concerned about a kidnapping attempt, but it's nothing concrete, only general concern based on crime in the countries we are visiting. If we can convince Cassie and Case to join ship-sponsored excursions with us or to take us with them to the orphanages Cassie wants to sponsor, they can have more guards around when they are off ship."

"Do you think kidnappers would try something on board?" asked Elle.

"Assuming they could get on board, they'd be stupid to. There are too many cameras. The only place we can't watch them is inside their suite. Which is why we have an extra camera on the hallway. As much fun as it was to watch the two of you play three rounds of mini golf, we don't need to guard them so close. On the same deck is good enough for an emergency response."

"So we need to become their friends but not keep eyes on them."

"They need eyes in crowded places like the dance clubs, bars, and casinos—not so much at the pool or in the theater." Jethro finished his meal and pushed his plate back. "Best tortillas I've had in years."

Melanie set her fork down. "There are no cameras in the bathrooms or in sections of the spa, just on the doors. Cassie has a spa appointment on our next at-sea day, Wednesday. Elle, ship security is going to book you an appointment at the same time. You may not have eyes on her at all times, but if you get chatting over a mani-pedi, you might end up talking most of the time."

"I can do a spa day. They won't make me take my earrings out, will they? I'd like to communicate if necessary, and I am sure phones aren't welcome."

"We haven't tested the earrings on board yet. I'm not sure how well they'll work. Colin was worried they might have issues with the ship's communications network." Alan took a drink of his water and coughed. He forgot about the bubbles.

"Let's go back to the ship early. I'll let security know we are testing a device so they can tell us if they have a problem on their end." Jethro stacked the plates in the center of the table. "Give us a ten-minute start. We will meet you at the lounge on deck 8."

Before they left port, Alan texted Colin the results of the hide-and-seek game he and ZoElle played most of the afternoon in testing the communications equipment. The biggest glitch was that when she turned on the earrings, a small pop could be heard on the ship's security radios. As they had guessed, the lower in the ship ZoElle went, the harder it was to pinpoint which deck she was on. They often ended up a level below or above her when using the locator. The audio was decent, although ZoElle had a hard time hearing unless she pressed the earring to a spot behind her ear.

The ship's security chief cleared the earrings for emergency use.

Alan counted it as a successful day, even if ZoElle had once again commandeered the couch.

CASE COULDN'T LET THE SEASICK incident go. Elle cringed as he slapped Alan on the back again and made an off-color comment about the situation, his behavior intensifying with each drink.

The ten-hour long excursion in Puerto Vallarta had sapped her energy, but she kept the smile on her face despite the ache in her feet. Who wanted to go dancing after a long day? The real newlyweds should have been hibernating, not drinking and dancing. When she did go on a real honeymoon, it would not be a cruise. The at-sea days were relaxing, but the two back-to-back port days, not so much. Cabo wasn't bad, they hadn't tried to keep up with tours or visit three orphanages in six hours as they did today in Puerto Vallarta.

Alan led her out on the dance floor while Case and Cassie danced. "Good beat for a cha-cha. Are you up to it?"

Elle forgot all about her tired feet as they took a few experimental steps to get into the rhythm before Alan guided her into her first spin. Other couples stepped back, giving them room. If she'd known for the last eighteen months that Alan could dance like this, she would have … done absolutely nothing. Alan wouldn't have dated her then, and he wouldn't once this assignment was over. And going dancing, no matter what you called it, spelled d-a-t-e.

When the song ended, Alan led her toward the table where the other newlyweds sat together in a single chair. Case leaned around Cassie. "And now for two days at sea. Can y'all handle it? I could write you a stronger prescription."

Alan's tight smile pierced Elle's heart. "He'll be fine. The patches are working. Every honeymoon should have something to laugh about in twenty years. What are you going to laugh about?" She kissed Alan on the cheek before sitting down next to him.

"We are still working on that." Case kissed Cassie's bare shoulder.

"Where did you learn to dance like that?" asked Cassie, apparently used to her husband's displays of affection.

"We both learned at school. You can't imagine how excited I was to learn Alan danced too." Elle took a sip of the water the waiter set on the table.

"So romantic. Just like Cinderella." Cassie turned to her husband. "We should take the ballroom class they're offering tomorrow afternoon."

"I thought we'd do a different kind of dancing." Case kissed Cassie for an uncomfortably long time.

Elle locked eyes with Alan. He lifted her hand and kissed her knuckles. So far, they had avoided kissing in public. Since their Sunday morning discussion of how Alan had gotten the bruise on his jaw, he'd struggled to relax when more than their hands touched. The dance must have helped. At some point, there would be another kiss. Elle concluded it would be easier to deal with if kissing were a regular occurrence. The anticipation? Downright dangerous. Her theory wasn't one she was going to suggest, though. If she was wrong, the awkwardness would only increase. There were only so many ways to avoid each other in their stateroom.

The music changed to a slow ballad, one of Elle's favorites. Alan and Elle stood in unison, and Cassie pulled Case to his feet.

"Y'all, I've got an idea. Let's change partners this once. I know my girl is dying to dance with you." Case's drawl had grown more pronounced with each drink.

Alan raised an eyebrow. Elle dropped her hold on his hand. "Sure, it will be fun."

Alan waltzed Cassie around the edge of the floor in a basic America style waltz step. Case grabbed Elle's hand, and they wound past several couples to the center of the floor. He put his hands on her waist and started to sway. Elle put her hands on his biceps to force some distance between them. No wonder Cassie had wanted to dance with Alan. Case danced like a middle-school boy. A couple bumped into Elle, causing her to step closer to Case. His hands drifted lower, and he pulled Elle against him, but she pushed back, regaining some distance.

"Oh, come on, babe, you know you want to dance this way. That man of yours doesn't understand what dancing is for." Case pulled her tight against him again and moved his hands to cup her bottom.

Shock reverberated through her body. Dr. Johnson had only been married for four days. And as far as he knew, so had she. "Remove your hands."

"Oh, so polite." He moved his hands back to her hips.

"Farther."

His hands crept up past her waist.

Elle stepped on his foot.

"Hey, why did you do that?"

"In case you missed the memo, I'm not your bride." Elle couldn't push herself any farther away as the other couples had boxed them in, all of them doing the same type of grinding dance Case was trying to do.

When his hands began to wander again, Elle dug her thumbs under his collarbone, and he stopped moving, "Dr. Johnson, do you know how many pounds of pressure the average woman puts on the spike of her high heels?"

"Um, no."

"A total of 240. I assume you know the damage that much weight can do?"

Case stepped back. "Where did you learn that?"

"Basic self-defense. It's taught in every class in the country."

"You know self-defense?"

"I'm famous for one thing. So, yes, I've learned self-defense." Every woman should know some. Does Cassie?"

"But you're rich, right? You had a bodyguard."

"I had a kind benefactor who wanted to protect me from a media storm I didn't start." Nick Gooding more than lived up to his name. Not only had he sent Alan to rescue her from the media parked in her front yard, he'd taken care of selling her old house, relocating her, and paid for an amazing therapist outside of her medical insurance coverage.

Case leaned his head closer. "How did you afford your suite on the trip?"

"Alan's sister paid for it."

"So she's rich?"

Alarm bells went off inside Elle's head. Not only was Case dancing inappropriately with another man's new wife, he wasn't listening to his own. Case had been there during the conversation where they'd discussed Abbie paying for the trip. "My sister-in-law has enough to be generous."

"Is that why you married him? Family money?"

"No."

Case yanked her flush against his body again, trapping her arms. Elle forced herself not to react. If she injured him, it would make her job impossible.

His alcohol-laced breath rolled across her ear like that of the evil dragon in the movies. "Well, he sure isn't giving you the right moves. There's no hunger when you look at each other. You barely touch. I bet this is the closest you've been to a man since he barfed all over you." He let go, pushed her out of stomping range, and laughed as the song ended. "If you need a real man, Cassie will be in the spa from nine till noon tomorrow."

Elle pushed through the crowd back to the table, where Cassie laughed with Alan. Elle dug up her actress smile and tucked herself into Alan's side. Right now, she wanted to be held by someone who could erase the feel of Case's hands. She'd have to settle for a half hug from Alan and a shower when the evening finally ended.

Carrying two drinks, Case arrived at the table a full two minutes after ZoElle did. She stiffened for a moment against Alan, her smile forced. Alan studied the doctor for a clue as to what had happened. His demeanor hadn't changed. Case leaned over, kissing his wife's neck, then held the glass in front of her.

Cassie took the glass and set it on the table. "I told you I don't want anything more to drink tonight. You don't need anything either."

Case hugged his wife from behind and drank over her shoulder, swaying to the beat of the music as he did so.

ZoElle tapped Alan's back in time to the music. "Dance with me?"

The crowd on the dance floor had swelled, leaving little room for the kind of dancing Alan preferred, so he held Elle in his arms and danced a box step.

She looked up at him and smiled. "Thank you."

"For what?"

"Dancing with me."

Alan raised a brow. He'd seen that look last year when ZoElle had been given her first full-time assignment and hadn't wanted to be the one to tell him. She was hiding something. "Do I want to know what happened during your dance with the doctor?"

She leaned her head on his shoulder. "No, but you need to know. I'll tell you in our room."

They finished the song in silence. Two empty glasses sat at their table when they returned. Alan scanned the room but didn't see the tall doctor. He checked his phone. Cassie's bodyguards noted the couple had returned to their suite. "Looks like we're off duty."

"Can we walk around the deck before we go in?"

Alan led ZoElle to the nearest door, trying not to run into anyone. Once they were in the open, he laid his arm across her shoulders. Her arm came around his waist. Alan walked slowly, wanting the moment to last. As soon as they entered their room, they would become polite friends again. Not touching or discussing anything beyond work. They would politely argue that the other person should have the luxury of the bed for the night and end up taking turns. They stopped at the railing and watched the moonlight dance on the ocean.

ZoElle sighed and leaned back against his chest. "I threatened to break Case's foot."

"What did he do?"

Waves crashed against the ship.

"Among other things, he insulted your manhood."

"What other things?"

"If he wasn't a client, I would have done more than step-on-his-foot-type things."

Alan turned ZoElle around so he could look in her eyes and waited for a better answer.

"Very suggestive dancing, which was mostly surprising since he's only been married five days—or is it four?" Elle counted on her fingers. "Four. This assignment seems longer…"

"What else happened?"

"He offered to fill in for you as my husband."

Tension tightened Alan's jaw and shoulders. If it were any other man on the ship, Alan would be pounding on his door and threatening him.

ZoElle ran her hands up and down his arms. "Relax. If it had been a single guy trying to pick me up at a club, I would have expected the behavior. And I would have stepped on his foot and left. But leaving didn't seem like a choice. I wanted to know how far he'd take it."

"I don't want to relax. I want to—"

She rested her hands on his shoulders. "We can't alienate them because he doesn't hold his liquor well."

"Doing nothing isn't an option either."

"What would Adam do to someone who hit on September? Or Alex if it was Kimberly?"

Several scenarios, most with Case and a bloody nose, came to mind. His muscles tightened again.

"Forget your brothers. What would your dad do if this happened to Melanie or Abbie?"

All the air in his lungs rushed out. "Dad would have a very intimidating man-to-man talk with the reprobate."

"Then that's what you should do. I'm going to see if I can get Cassie to talk at the spa. I'm not sure what to tell her. What if Case says I came on to him?"

Alan pulled her in for a hug. "I could drop him overboard. If we are lucky, there will be sharks."

ZoElle laughed against his chest, and the sound reverberated through him. It was the first genuine laugh he'd heard from her in days.

He rubbed her back as she continued to laugh. "Or maybe a giant squid."

"Stop. I'm laughing so hard my eyes are leaking."

Stepping back, Alan released the hug. The Sassy Seniors, dressed in coordinating blue shirts declaring they were old enough to know better and young enough to not care, rushed up.

"Don't you look adorable!"

"Have you been dancing?"

"Oh, good. You're wearing your seasick patch." The last one was Linda.

Alan couldn't remember the other names. "I'm feeling much better. Thank you for your help the other night."

ZoElle dropped her hands from his shoulders. "Have you been enjoying your cruise?"

"I would be if Georgia would stop winning all the bingo prizes."

"Considering your standing in the bridge tournament, you shouldn't complain."

"We enjoyed Cabo more than Puerto Vallarta. The tour guide for our excursion couldn't answer any of our questions."

"We won't ask how you are enjoying your cruise. We can see." The ladies giggled. ZoElle's blush bloomed.

"We need to take a selfie. I must put them in my scrapbook." The shortest woman produced a selfie stick and expertly attached it to her camera.

"Linda, you stand next to our handsome hunk, Pat and Georgia on the other side of Elle." The short one handed the selfie stick to Linda. "I have a bad angle. You try."

"Everyone smile!" The light on the phone flashed.

"They should have been kissing."

"Ooh, so cute. Lay one on her."

Alan looked to ZoElle for permission. They'd made it this far without kissing. She moved closer, and he met her halfway, their lips pressed together for the camera.

"That isn't a real kiss," Georgia scolded.

"You can do better," said Annie.

As Alan angled his head for the second kiss, ZoElle's lips parted, and her hands came up around his neck. Lights flashed. Someone tapped him on the shoulder.

"We're done now. You can come up for air."

Reluctantly, Alan ended the kiss to see ZoElle's blush. He hoped some lucky man would appreciate her blushes.

"We'll be on our way. You kids have better things to do than talk to old ladies all night."

"They could make cruise babies."

ZoElle buried her head in his shoulder as the women moved off. "I'm going to die of embarrassment."

"Mom claims that isn't possible." Although it might be possible to drown in one of ZoElle's kisses.

"Do you think the cucumbers do anything?" asked Elle.

Cassie answered in a sleepy voice from the lounge chair to Elle's right. "They remove puffiness and dark circles, although on vacation, I've been sleeping more than usual."

"I've always thought they were so we couldn't see each other with our faces covered with mud."

"Don't make me laugh. My face will crack."

"Since I have cucumbers on my eyes, I won't see it."

Cassie laughed. "There, you did it. My face just cracked. If Case doesn't think I'm beautiful still, I'm blaming you."

Elle answered while trying to keep her tightening face from moving. "If he thinks less of you because your facial cracked, he needs to have his eyes examined."

The instrumental music flowed around them, the scent of the essential oils permeating the air. Several minutes passed before Cassie spoke again. "Is marriage what you thought it would be?"

"You mean all five days of it? The honeymoon isn't over if that's what you mean." Could this be an opening to tell Cassie about her dance with Case?

"I don't know what I mean. Maybe it's the cruise. Case seems interested in partying and the bedroom. We aren't talking as much. Even when we visited the orphanages. Is Alan like that?"

"We do plenty of talking still." Not really, but telling Cassie she was on her tenth book since starting the cruise wasn't an option. Or that compared to Alan, Mr. Darcy was loquacious. And they had talked more on the ship than they had the entire month of January after her promotion.

"Maybe I'm insecure. I feel like things aren't the same, like he isn't interested in my mind anymore."

Interesting. Perhaps telling Cassie about Case's inappropriate dance wouldn't be helpful. "It's our honeymoon. Conventional wisdom says there isn't nearly as much talking on a honeymoon as before."

"I guess you're right."

The soft footsteps of an attendant interrupted them.

Three hours later, polished, massaged, and glowing, Cassie and Elle left the spa.

"We should head down to the pastry counter or get a gelato before we go find our husbands."

Cassie looked at the time on her phone. "He isn't expecting me for another half hour. Just don't tell Case I went with you. He's warned me not to gain the 'cruise fifteen.'"

Everything Elle had read in Cassie's file showed she was an independent, savvy businesswoman. Why would she let Case dictate her life? Maybe it was a new-bride thing. But then, Elle hadn't cut her hair short because Abbie said Alan liked girls with long hair. "I figure I can always spend an extra ten minutes on the treadmill if I need to."

They headed toward the shops and started down the grand staircase. Cassie grabbed Elle's arm as her gaze locked on the cybercafé. "I need to go back to my room."

Case stood near the café entrance speaking to a male crew member. Though they couldn't hear him, it was obvious from his stance that he was upset. Elle followed Cassie back up the stairs and to the nearest elevator bank. They didn't speak again until they neared their staterooms.

"It was good to go to the spa with a friend." Cassie pulled her key card out of her shorts pocket.

Elle studied her fingernails. "We should do another mani-pedi next week. My nails will be trash in two days."

"I'd like that. I talked Case into the ballroom class after lunch. Maybe we can go to dinner together after?"

"I'll ask Alan." Elle pulled out her own key card.

Cassie disappeared into her room first.

Housekeeping had finished with Elle's suite, the towel elephants a huge giveaway. Although her favorite was the monkeys on Tuesday. One had been drinking from the sparkling-cider bottle.

She completed a sweep of the rooms. Alan must not have been in since housekeeping had finished. She opened the Hastings app and tapped out a message to Melanie.

Need advice. Where can we talk? No men.

—I want one of those macarons. Meet you at the bakery counter. Headed there now.

Elle walked the long way around her deck so she didn't have to pass Cassie's door. The elevator pinged as she neared it.

Case exited and blocked her way. "Y'all finished already?"

"Barely." The elevator door closed before she could get on.

"Where's Cassie?"

"In your suite, I believe."

"Where is your adoring husband?" Case looked around the empty lobby.

Elle twisted the lower bead on her dangling earring. The wire hook didn't bite into her neck like during the test. Colin wanted as much wire as possible to help boost the signal. The faint pop of the comms turning on echoed in her ear. "I'm going to meet him."

"Dressed like that?" Case advanced a step.

Her knee-length shorts and shirt combo was appropriate for most of the daytime ship activities. "Obviously."

He put his hand on the wall behind her, trapping her. "Over-dressed for a workout? I didn't peg you as the type."

"I just had my nails done. I plan on skipping the workout and watching Alan. If you'll excuse me."

Case grabbed her arm. "Not so fast. I wanted to apologize. I do stupid things when I am drunk, and last night I stepped way over the line with you."

"You should apologize to Cassie." Elle slipped free of his grasp.

"You didn't tell her, did you?" Panic filled his face. Good. He should be worried.

"It didn't come up, but if you touch me again ..." She let the threat hang as she ducked around him and pushed the elevator button. Please, no empty elevator. The elevator pinged, and the doors slid open. Alan stepped off, his T-shirt damp with sweat. "There you are, dear."

Case hurried down the hallway toward his room.

Elle turned off the comms. "Great timing."

Alan walked her to the suite and opened the door.

"So, what was that all about?"

"You mean my call for help? Apparently a bit premature. I wouldn't want to be his patient. His manner is appalling." Elle sat down on the end of the bed.

Alan pulled a clean shirt out of the closet. "I talked with him this morning. Apparently he got the message."

"He could use a bit more humility. As apologies go, his was pretty lame."

Alan grunted. "I'm going to shower. I'll find you after your meeting with my mom. I want a macaron too."

Sweet brownie bites. She hadn't sent the message on private mode. Elle jumped up. "I'm late."

Melanie was tapping her chin and staring into the bakery counter as she waved someone ahead of her.

"Can't decide?" asked Elle.

"They all look too rich. Maybe a turn around the deck first."

Elle followed her out the nearest door. They found a spot along the railing with no one near.

"Interesting conversation you had with the doctor."

"You heard?"

Melanie tapped her hearing aid. "This isn't only for show, you know."

"I hadn't realized. But it makes sense. Alan doesn't have a receiver other than his phone and sunglasses."

"Much more convenient. Now, what did you need to talk about?"

Elle repeated her conversation with Cassie. "Given that side of Case and her insecurities, I'm surprised she married him. Was there something I missed in the files? Dr. Johnson's was rather thin."

"It was a whirlwind courtship, which is why we didn't have more lead time. I don't know how much of a background check they were able to do on him. I can ask Peter and Zane if they have more. Dr. Johnson only returned from working in Africa in November. After watching my own children, I don't think love follows a timeline. Then there are so many adjustments to be made getting used to another person. You may be seeing things that aren't there."

Twirling the end of her ponytail around her finger, Elle analyzed her thoughts. "Case propositioned me last night."

"Alan told me that. He was concerned you weren't detailed enough about it."

"I don't want Alan slugging him." Elle focused on the sliver of coastline in the distance.

"That bad?"

"If I'd given him more than a general idea, he might have gone all protector on me. I can take care of myself. I don't want to alienate Cassie. And Case was definitely drunk."

Melanie placed her hand on top of Elle's. "Promise me that if Case goes too far, you won't hesitate to show him some of your best defense techniques. It isn't worth you getting hurt."

"I will. Right now, I want him to think of me as a victim who's had a self-defense class. He is more likely to let me hang around Cassie if I'm not a real threat."

"He could be coming on to you, so you don't want to be around Cassie." Melanie stared out to sea.

"I hadn't thought of that." Elle's phone pinged. "Alan is looking for me."

"What's the actual story behind Alan's bruised chin? Are you two doing all right on this assignment?"

"The shot they gave him for seasickness made him woozy. I tried to help him to bed and ended up in a position that triggered me. I hit him before my brain realized I was safe. He doesn't remember much of it. There has been a lot of apologizing on both sides. I should answer his text." Anything to not elaborate on the fact that the only time they'd relaxed around each other was dancing last night. And the kiss with the seniors. That had been enough to keep her from sleeping well last night. From the amount of movement she'd heard from the bedroom, she knew Alan hadn't slept well either. Her life had become some distorted movie, where the woman portraying her wasn't attracted to the man she was hired to act like she was attracted to. Meanwhile, the man who was pretending to be attracted to her wasn't attracted to her. Unless he had enough drugs to down a small whale, in which case he became talkative and called her pretty. Her movie would never be a box-office hit.

"So, are you two all right?"

"I think so."

Alan walked along the railing toward them.

"We'll see you two later." Melanie headed off in the direction of the bakery.

Elle took a deep breath and reached for Alan's hand. Case might back off if he observed a more loving relationship.

Dressed in poodle skirts, the ever-matching Sassy Seniors entered the dance floor of the closed bar and waved at Alan. Today's shirt was yellow and announced they'd "Been there, done that" in Antarctica.

The ladies in the ballroom firmly tipped the numbers of females to males. Cassie and Case entered last. A man stood in the doorway. Alan couldn't see who it was from his vantage point, so he tried to get ZoElle to go to the door for a closer look, but the man disappeared. Alan caught a flash of white—maybe it was a crew member checking on things.

One of the four crew members teaching the class raised his hand to get everyone's attention. "Welcome to our beginning ballroom class. Most of you brought a partner—including partners who don't want to be here. Remember, the gelato she bribed you with is included in your fare."

Nervous laughter came from several sections of the room, and the instructor continued his introduction. Another employee walked over to ZoElle and Alan. He led them away from the rest of the group. "You two were the ones dancing in the club last night, right?"

"Yes."

"Would you mind joining us for the demonstration? We play about a minute each of several styles of music and let them watch people dancing to show ballroom dancing isn't about everyone doing the same thing at the same time."

"We aren't that good," said ZoElle.

"I was behind the bar last night, and you are better than good."

Alan looked to ZoElle. He agreed they were good enough to dance an impromptu exhibition, but he didn't want to embarrass her. ZoElle's bright eyes and smile convinced him to agree.

The employee handed them a piece of paper. "This is the order we play the songs. If you don't want to do one, just stand on the sidelines."

"I wish I'd worn one of my other skirts. This one isn't very twirly."

"Twirly?" asked Alan.

"You know what I mean." She held out the blue skirt to show it wasn't as full as the one she wore last night.

Alan tucked ZoElle's hand into his. "I like the color." He stopped himself before explaining that the color reflected the gray in her eyes and reminded him of a storm over Lake Michigan. It was probably best not to notice things like her eyes.

The instructor turned to Alan and ZoElle. "Some of you may have seen this couple dance last night. They have agreed to join us in demonstrating the dances. Although the basic steps are the same, the styling can vary from couple to couple."

Alan walked ZoElle onto the floor and waited for the music to start. As before, once they were dancing, the world fell away, and nothing but ZoElle existed for Alan. He hadn't enjoyed dancing so much since he'd unsuccessfully attempted to catch the eye of a little redheaded coed.

The demonstration ended with thunderous clapping, especially from their friends the senior women. Linda put her pinkie fingers in her mouth and whistled. ZoElle curtsied as he bowed.

"Thank you very much for your help. You're welcome to stay if you want, but you obviously don't need this class." The instructor seemed to want them to leave.

"Thank you so much for allowing us to dance." ZoElle bobbed her head and tugged on Alan's arm.

As soon as they rounded the corner, Alan stopped. "Why are we leaving? We can't watch them if we don't stay."

"We will also intimidate the other students. And it looks weird to hang around when you are better than either of the instructors. There is only one exit, so we change up our strategy."

She had a point. "How?"

"I counted six cameras in there. We can have them watched from afar, and we can run into them at dinner. Your parents can stroll by when the class is finished."

Alan tapped the request into his phone and received confirmation. "So, now what?"

"I don't know about you, but I've come this close"—ZoElle held up her thumb and forefinger nearly pinched together—"to eating either gelato or a macaron today and been denied. And that is all my brain can think about. I'm going down to get one or both before I go crazy."

"I didn't realize treats were so important to you." Alan followed her down the corridor.

"A woman's got to have her chocolate." She laughed. "Don't look at me that way. I'm not going to force you to eat any of it."

"What way?"

"The this-doesn't-compute-because-the-data-isn't-in-binary-code way." She pushed the button for the elevator.

"I don't think in code." They stepped into the empty elevator.

ZoElle tapped the center of his chest with her index finger. "Yes, you do. Zero or one, off or on, black or white. Your mind is running as fast as it can trying to figure out how I can think of eating when we just had lunch. And you're right. Chocolate isn't hunger, it's a craving. Don't you ever have cravings?"

Right now he was having a very inappropriate craving for her lips. The elevator camera blinked its red eye at him, reminding him there would be digital evidence if he gave in to this craving. Where were the Sassy Seniors and their selfie stick when he needed them? "I do—for Wrigley Field hot dogs."

"I don't think they have those on board."

The doors opened.

ZoElle took his hand.

Alan was still thinking about her lips. "You never know. They could have the best dogs on the high seas."

"I've never heard of a ship known for hot dogs. But they are known for their chocolate."

Alan added chocolate to his list of things to make ZoElle happy.

12

Captain Wagner cordially invites
Alan & ZoElle Hastings
to dine with him Thursday at 7:30 p.m.
Please meet at 7:00 p.m. on deck 8 forward elevators for
cocktails in the Captain's Cabin before being escorted to dinner.
Dress: formal, or suit and tie

ELLE SHOWED THE CARD TO Alan before answering the cruise's social director, whom she'd invited into the suite. "We would be honored to go."

"Thank you. Does either of you have any food allergies?"

Alan shook his head.

"No. However, neither of us drinks alcohol."

The social director smiled. "Not to worry. I'll make sure your glasses are filled with the nonalcoholic version. One of the other couples we've invited doesn't drink either."

"Thank you."

Alan closed the door after the director left. "I wonder where Cassie and Case will be dining."

Elle checked the Hastings app. "With us and your parents."

"That explains the other nondrinking couple."

"I hope they won't put me next to Case." Elle had made it a point not to sit next to him since the incident at the elevator yesterday.

"I've been making sure you don't."

"The seating arrangements are made by the social director. They break up the married couples so everyone has a chance to visit."

The scowl on Alan's face mirrored her feelings. "Can you put in a request?"

Elle turned the invitation over. "I don't think I should. If he gets handsy, I'll dump my drink in his lap."

Alan's rich laughter filled the suite.

"I'm serious."

"I know. I'm getting my laughter out now so I don't laugh at the table."

Elle rolled her eyes.

"One problem. I don't have my tux."

Elle opened the closet and pulled out a tux. "Abbie had me pack this for you. She said you'd decide you could get away with one of your work suits."

"Good thing. I don't think my tux would have survived getting on the plane." Alan took the tux and laid it across the bed. "Thanks for bringing it. Anything else my sister had you pack for me?"

"Other than the matching T-shirts for celebrating one week of marriage? No." If he hadn't discovered the silk boxers in his drawer yet, she wasn't going to embarrass either of them by mentioning them. So far, she'd fixed their room each morning without using them or any other of the not-ripped lacy items Abbie had given her. Feeling a blush creep up her face, Elle turned to face her dress choices for the evening.

"Do we have to wear the matching shirts tomorrow?"

Biting her cheek, Elle suppressed a laugh at the whine in his voice. "Long enough to get a photo for Abbie."

"She will hold the photos hostage. You have no idea what she could do with them."

"She wouldn't do that."

Alan scrolled through his phone. "Cassie and Case haven't left their room yet. It's nearly noon. Are we sure they are there?"

"Did they answer the door when the social director delivered their invitation?" Elle debated between two dresses for the evening. She wanted to wear the green one as it would be a dream to dance in, but the floor to midthigh slit hidden by the ruffle would not work if she were seated next to Case. The two-tone, single-shoulder blue dress would be less trouble, but after the compliment Alan had paid her yesterday about the color, she hesitated. The warmth hadn't been in his words. It was the look in his eyes that haunted her. She'd seen that same look on his brothers' faces when they gazed at their wives or fiancées. Alan hadn't allowed the emotion to stay long, maybe a half second, but she'd seen it. Abbie's prediction that Alan would love the blue didn't help. Despite any chemistry they might have, he'd made his position clear. They were at work, and nothing could happen between them, ever. Wearing the blue because she knew he liked it was something a real wife would do.

"Ready for lunch? The newlyweds have left their room."

Elle shut the closet. "Another meal? This job is spoiling me."

"Beats sneaking protein bars in the middle of a twelve-hour shift." He handed her the ship ID and scan card.

She took it without touching him or meeting his eyes. The food wasn't the only thing spoiling her. And like going back to protein bars, the thought of giving up this pretend romantic life didn't sound very appealing.

Three well-hidden cameras had been placed around the captain's cabin. Alan considered the one he'd noticed embedded in the shelf above an intricate ship in a bottle. He busied himself searching for other cameras to distract himself from the curve of ZoElle's neck and bare shoulder. Her dress was less revealing than the woman in red, some movie star who had been popular fifteen years ago, or even Cassie's low-backed one. But he didn't want to touch either of them. Fortunately, touching the back of ZoElle's neck had been forbidden during their meeting with Zoe. At the time, he hadn't thought wanting to touch her would be a problem, but it was far easier to see ZoElle as a coworker when she was in a suit or the company polo. She'd worn evening wear for red-carpet events when they'd needed a guard to blend in, but usually he'd been locked away in a command room or back at the office, overseeing multiple events.

Alan laid a protective hand at ZoElle's waist as Case approached without his wife.

"We can't seem to get away from y'all." Case's glare was for Alan only.

"It's because there are only 3,821 passengers on the ship. If there were an even four thousand, you'd never notice us." ZoElle leaned back into Alan's hand.

He slipped his arm around her waist and used his best "back-off" glare on Case.

The doctor ignored him. "You look ravishing in that dress, Elle."

ZoElle lifted her glass higher, blocking Case from getting closer, and turned to stare into Alan's eyes. "I'm glad you like it. The color matches my husband's eyes—my favorite color."

His heart missed a beat before speeding up. "I didn't know." The huskiness in his voice was good acting. Abbie would be proud.

"Really?" Her breathless whisper barely reached his ears. If he hadn't been watching her lips, he might have missed it.

As Alan lowered his head to meet ZoElle's lips, he told himself it was solely to drive home the back-off message. But judging from the way he instinctively pulled her closer and deepened the kiss, his brain failed to inform the rest of him that this was the purpose. It had only been two days since he'd last kissed her for the selfies with the seniors. His starved lips begged for more, and ZoElle—

Alan reluctantly ended the kiss when someone cleared their throat. The captain stood where Case had been, a huge grin on his face, the wrinkles around his eyes attesting to the humor the man often found in life.

ZoElle recovered first, dropping her hand from Alan's chest and turning to give their host one of her perfect smiles. "Captain Wagner, thank you for inviting us. I'm sorry, I didn't notice you standing there."

"It isn't the first time, Mrs. Hastings, I've had that effect on a pair of newlyweds and occasionally those celebrating their golden anniversary."

Alan extended his hand to shake the captain's.

"Mr. Hastings, it's nice to see newlyweds getting along. We'll talk more at dinner. I have a few more guests to meet." The captain moved on to the next couple, also addressing them by name—a trick he must use to keep the names in his short-term memory. Alan used the same say the name out loud trick often.

ZoElle sipped her drink. "We should mingle too."

Alan exchanged niceties with the six guests he didn't know. One woman and her husband were on their thirtieth cruise and their third time through the canal. He tried to focus on what was being said, but the kiss kept derailing his thoughts.

Finally, the social director indicated it was time to go to dinner. ZoElle took his arm, and they followed his parents out of the room. They entered the dining room via spiral staircase. As they reached the bottom of the stairs, someone announced each couple and what had brought them to the captain's table.

Alan was seated between his mother and the woman who'd been on thirty cruises. Across the table, ZoElle sat next to his father and the captain. Case sat at the far end of the table between the woman celebrating her golden anniversary and a female crew member. ZoElle was safe for now.

"The kiss you gave your wife reminded me of my husband when

we were younger." The woman continued to detail the locations where her husband had stolen inappropriate kisses.

Heat rose up the back of Alan's neck. Melanie unsuccessfully hid a laugh behind a cough. Finally, the captain started the dinner with a toast. Alan didn't care what the toast was for as long as the woman next to him started eating and talked less.

Why anyone would spend hundreds of dollars for a pair of high heels with a designer name baffled Elle. She waited impatiently for the elevator to reach their deck so she could lose the shoes. Focusing on the pain in her left small toe kept her from noticing the feeling of Alan's hand on her back. He'd been possessive of her the entire evening. Case seemed to have gotten the message because not once during dinner had he even looked her direction. Since getting into the elevator, he'd only had eyes, and hands, for his wife.

Elle focused on the numbers above the door, trying to ignore the whispering and giggles from the other corner of the elevator. Alan's fingers brushed across her bare shoulder and slid down her arm. His territorial show wasn't over. Elle focused on her left toe again. *And this little piggy went why, why, why all the way ...* There wasn't any place to go. The doors opened. Alan's hand moved to her waist. Cassie finger waved as she and Case disappeared into their suite.

Alan continued his charade until he closed the door and shut out the rest of the ship. "Do you want to use the bathroom first?"

The carpet felt cool against her aching feet. Elle picked up her shoes before answering. "I'd like to take a shower. Mr. Fiftieth Anniversary had something sticky on his hands when he danced with me." She'd actually already wiped the goo off in the lady's room, but she needed some alone time, and the bathroom was the only place she could be by herself. "You can change first."

He tugged on his bow tie and turned to the mirror above the dresser. "I hope my kiss wasn't too—"

Amazing, spontaneous, toe tingling? Elle walked over to the window and looked out to sea. This was not a conversation she needed. She'd managed to go all evening without analyzing the kiss for longer than a few seconds at a time. They had to have some chemistry to have their kisses explode like that.

Alan cleared his throat. "I wanted Case to back off. Sorry if I overstepped."

"It worked." She struggled to keep a neutral tone. "He got the message."

"I wanted to make sure you were okay. It was more intense than I planned." He opened and closed drawers and the closet door.

Too bad the stupid heels weren't on her feet anymore. She needed the pain to keep her from focusing on Alan dissecting a staged kiss her heart wanted to be real. "You did what was needed."

She didn't breathe again until the bathroom door was closed, separating them. The ocean failed to calm her as she drowned in her own stupidity. How had she thought she could do this job and not be affected? She should have known better last week at their fake wedding. She checked her phone. Yup, exactly one week ago tonight he'd planted the first devastating kiss on her lips—the one that made her wish she was a real bride. Ten days. She could do ten more days. Then she'd spend a week with her parents in Tampa before returning to Chicago. Only, a week wouldn't be enough. She hadn't gotten over her crush in a year of trying. Somewhere deep inside a hidden, encrypted file, she'd even kept a list of every flaw, every annoying thing Alan did, in hopes of killing the crush. Unfortunately, 90 percent of the time, she could attribute his actions to good motives. Like his analyzing tonight's kiss, as annoying as that was, showed he was trying to watch out for his work partner and adhere to the guidelines they'd set.

Last month, Deidre had said Dermot Security was still search-ing for female guards. Elle wouldn't have to move from her apart-ment, and the pay was about the same. And at the events where she would cross work with Hastings, Alan was always behind the monitors. She could go months without seeing any of the broth-ers. Tomorrow, when they were ashore in Guatemala, she could text Deidre and have her ask Liam. Then she could give her two weeks' notice to Melanie and Jethro. Once she stepped off the ship in Miami, she'd never have to see Alan again. Or she could return to her old career. She'd had job offers, but that was in a world she wasn't ready to reenter. It would be too easy to hide behind a computer and never interact with people. Looking back over her career, she realized that not interacting with others had been her biggest flaw. Oddly enough, being too focused and an inability to completely let go of the ordered digital portion of his life were flaws in Alan she adored.

She felt more than heard Alan come up behind her before she caught his reflection in the window. The soft gray T-shirt he had changed into accentuated his shoulders. He stood behind her for a moment, watching the sea. "I'm going to meet up with Dad while you're in the shower."

Elle nodded, unable to answer him.

"Are you sure you're okay?"

"I'm fine."

He stepped closer until his hand hovered above her shoulder, warmth radiating from his palm, but his hand dropped before he touched her. He smelled more of soap than of the aftershave he'd worn to dinner. She preferred this version of him. "I'm really sorry I got carried away with the kiss. It won't happen again."

He seemed to be studying her reflection in the glass as much as she was his. What was the point of keeping her back to him when he could see her reactions? "I know. We're good."

The silence between them grew, the loudest noise in the room the wind swirling outside the ship.

"ZoElle?"

"Just Elle." Although correcting him did no good. He'd never get it right.

He looked like he was going to say something, but then he shook his head and turned away. At the door, he stopped. "I'll be back in forty-five minutes or so."

She raised her hand to indicate she'd heard. Enough time to shower and pretend to fall asleep on the couch so she could avoid him until morning.

ALAN FOUND HIS FATHER IN a small lobby, seated behind a chess table. A pawn was missing from the set.

"I'm assuming your pawn jumped ship."

Dad held up a penny. "Use this and tell me what's on your mind."

He took the coin. "A new version of 'a penny for your thoughts?'"

"Something like that." Jethro moved his pawn to start play.

Alan pretended to study the board as he planned out what he wanted to ask his father and what he wanted to tell him. He moved a pawn and remained silent.

They played until Jethro captured a bishop. "Your mind isn't on the game."

"I think I blundered tonight, and I don't know how to make things right."

"What did you do?" A silent *now* ended his father's question.

"I kissed ZoElle."

"The kiss in front of the captain? A rather convincing kiss. That should keep Case from bothering her."

"That's the problem. I didn't kiss her to warn off Case. I mean I did, but I didn't. I wanted to kiss her. Case just gave me an excuse."

Jethro's hand hovered over his knight. "So you kissed her because you wanted to?"

"Basically."

Jethro moved.

Alan ran a hand through his hair before capturing his father's knight, realizing too late that he'd opened up his queen.

"And this is a problem?"

"We're friends. She's my client. I'm supposed to protect her."

"Elle *was* your principal. She isn't anymore. She's your work partner and friend."

"You're the one who says 'Once a client, always under our protection.'"

"I was referring to September and Jordan, who both required continuing protection, clients we couldn't abandon. Elle doesn't need our protection anymore." Dad held up his hand. "Yes, Mr. Gooding hires security for her when she goes on a talk show with his wife, for crowd control."

His father hadn't seen her cowering behind the kitchen island and hugging her knees. Or the look of horror on her face when she'd seen him through the window of her back door. Or her face the other night when he—did whatever he did.

Jethro captured a rook. "She isn't a woman who needs a guard anymore. She hasn't been for a long time."

"What?"

"Elle. She isn't the same person she was the day you extracted her from her home and rescued her from the media storm."

Alan moved his king. "I never said she was."

"I reread your files from when she was your client. I don't think you gave her enough credit even then."

"What do you mean?" Alan pushed back from the table. His next move would be his last. The game was lost.

"Did you know that for years, your mom has volunteered at the hospital as a victim advocate? She sits with victims as they go through up to six hours of questions and an invasive collection of evidence. Your mom provides them with clean clothes and a ride to someplace safe as well as contact with a rape crisis center. To hear Melanie explain it, the reporting process is more traumatic to some than the crime. Not all police or medical personal are as kind as they should be. The questions cast doubt on the victim. In those hospitals without advocates, victims are sent home wearing a pair of scrubs or clothes from the lost and found. Many women don't report their assaults because they've heard nightmarish stories about the process. Or they fear the unthinkable—that their attack will become public knowledge."

All he'd ever thought about this was the occasional five-minute scene in a TV police show. Hours?

"Elle was in a small town. Her attacker was a bigwig in her company. I don't know if she had an advocate. A week later, she was on national TV, completely composed and discussing how the media had irresponsibly turned her life upside down when they not only used her name in their broadcasts but misreported the identity of her attacker. Her life turned so far upside down she required new employment and the anonymity Chicago offered to rebuild her life. Not only did she go from being the woman you described on the floor of her kitchen to one of the best bodyguards we have at Hastings, she's become an advocate for other victims. You look at Elle and see a victim in need of protection. I see a survivor turned protector."

"But she was—"

Jethro held a thumb drive in his hand. "This has all the national TV coverage she was on with Zoe Gooding as well as a question-and-answer she does with the self-defense class she taught last fall and a few other things. Plead food poisoning or something and take tomorrow to watch this. Your mom and I will take Elle with us on our excursion, tailing Cassie and Case."

"But I need—"

"You need to stop babying your partner. I wish I realized how bad things were weeks ago when you objected to her promotion."

"She wasn't ready."

"Watch the videos. Now, are you going to move that piece so we can finish this game?"

Alan made the only move he could.

"Checkmate."

The stars hung low over the ocean. Sitting in one of the chaise lounges on the balcony, Elle typed the questions she wanted to ask Dermot Security into her phone. Since their biggest client was Harmon Media, they might want to put her on Abbie Harmon's security team, and while she liked Abbie, she didn't want to risk running into Alan. It wasn't exactly a request one could make of their next employer: "Please make sure I don't see my old boss." Not a good one for her industry. She could ask Peter if the firm he worked for in Dallas needed bodyguards. If only Dallas wasn't so hot half the year. Jethro and Melanie had contacts in Seattle. Andrew was creating a branch of Hastings in California. She worked well with Andrew.

But he had the Hastings's blue eyes.

And Alan would probably call Andrew's office.

Harmon Media often had celebrities or famous models onsite who had privately contracted with Hastings. Her best bet was Dermot Security. After a few months, she was bound to forget Alan, especially if he wasn't talking in her earpiece every other hour.

After checking the time, Elle tucked her phone into the pocket of her hoodie. She should move to the couch so Alan would think she was sleeping when he returned. There was just enough time to watch the sea for a few more minutes.

The lamp in the sitting area was on, and the couch was empty. Maybe ZoElle was finally giving him a turn on the couch. Alan set the macarons he'd bought next to the coffee maker. The bedroom door was open. Good. He needed to brush his teeth.

The bed was still made. Alan checked the Hastings app. No messages. Her earrings weren't activated. Only the lingering scent of her citrus shampoo proved she'd been in the bathroom. ZoElle could give Abbie lessons on keeping her makeup out of the way when sharing a bathroom—although he'd long suspected Abbie left makeup on every surface just to annoy him and his brothers and to get the bedroom with the private bath after the remodel.

The blue evening dress hung in the closet. He'd been only twenty minutes later than he'd planned. ZoElle wouldn't have gone to look for him, would she?

The sea breeze whistled through a crack where the balcony door wasn't shut. Alan went to close the sliding glass door and saw something flutter on one of the chairs. The blanket from the couch. Moonlight kissed ZoElle's cheeks and reflected off her still-damp hair. She didn't look up when he came out, and it took Alan a moment to realize she was asleep. He sat on the other chair and studied her, comparing her to the woman his father thought he had etched in his brain. The bruises she'd hidden under thick makeup on her face and neck when they'd first met had long since faded. By the time she'd started working for Hastings a month later, she'd sported the natural look he preferred.

What kind of idiot was he? He'd seen the bruises when she was in makeup prepping for one of the talk shows in New York. ZoElle had protested when the makeup artist had started removing the heavy layer of slime she'd worn on her face, revealing the yellow-and-green bruises around her left eye and along her jawline. Over the years, he'd had a few black eyes and hits to the jaw. He'd never thought about the fact that she might have been in physical pain the day they'd met. She may have even had a headache from the concussion.

She stirred in her sleep and pulled the blanket up to her chin. The temperature had dropped, nowhere near freezing but cool enough she shouldn't sleep out here all night.

Alan reached over and touched her knee. "ZoElle?"

Like all good bodyguards, she came fully alert. "Oh, I didn't mean to fall asleep out here." She swung her legs around and sat at the end of the lounge chair.

"Take the bed. You need a good night's sleep."

She gathered up her blanket. "We've discussed this. You are too tall for the couch. I am getting a decent sleep."

He followed her into the suite, where she tossed the blanket on the couch and retrieved her pillow from the bedroom. "Let me brush my teeth, and the room is all yours."

Alan kicked off his shoes and sat on the couch.

"Move. You're on my bed."

"It's my turn."

She placed both hands on her hips. "We both need to be at the top of our game to tag team with Cassie's detail tomorrow. If you sleep here, you'll wake up with cramps in your neck and back, and I won't sleep for guilt of you not sleeping."

Since he planned to stay on board tomorrow, he couldn't let her think she was the cause of his feigned illness. "And you don't think I have guilt?"

"Not much. I hear you snore." Her comment lightened his mood.

"I don't snore."

ZoElle held up her phone. "I can take a poll on the Hastings app."

"They'll lie just to be on your side." Alan stood. "You win tonight. Next sea day, it's mine."

"Why? Something is as likely to happen on board as it is on shore. You can't compromise the job because you are having another moment of misguided chivalry."

There wasn't much he could say to that. "Good night." Alan closed the bedroom door, giving them both some privacy.

ELLE ROLLED OFF THE COUCH and into several stretches. The couch was nowhere near as comfortable as she pretended. Alan would never find out, though. He thought too little of her already, and there was, as usual, no point in complaining. If not for the furnidents the fold-out bed would leave in the carpet, she'd fold it out at night, but there wouldn't be much point in her bedroom staging if housekeeping realized they weren't sharing a bed.

Seagulls screeched, and the ship ceased the hum she associated with the engines. She checked out the window. Either they'd docked early or she'd slept in. The clock on the wall confirmed both. Alan was usually up first. Elle tapped on the bedroom door. Silence. Maybe he was in the bathroom. She opened the door far enough to see he was still in bed. Shirtless. The light filtered through the window blinds highlighted the contours of his muscles, inviting her eyes to explore. *Sweet hot peppers*. Why now? He always wore a shirt, even in the swimming pool. The call to Deidre couldn't come soon enough. Her heart and hormones couldn't take much more of this job.

"Alan?"

He didn't move.

What to do? Her clothes were in the closet. Maybe he'd wake up if she made enough noise in the bathroom.

Ten minutes later, she emerged dressed for the day. Alan had rolled over so his back was to her. The sheets had slipped below his waist and were tangled with his Captain America sleep pants. "Alan? Time to get up. We are going to miss the excursion."

He raised up on one elbow and picked his phone up off the nightstand. *Double sweet hot peppers.* All the workouts he'd been doing to avoid her were showing. Elle moved to the sitting room, the dose of shirtless Alan enough for one day. The temperature outside was supposed to reach 32°C, which was somewhere in the low nineties. That didn't explain why she felt the need to fan herself in their temperature-controlled suite.

Alan appeared in the doorway, the missing shirt covering his abs. Shame. "I forgot to tell you last night. Dad asked me to stay on board and do some things. My cover story is that I'm sick. Probably something I ate."

"Oh. Will it look weird if I go without you?"

Alan shrugged. "If anyone asks, tell them I insisted you go have fun. Dad said he'd need you to tag team with them today guarding Cassie. Peter will be there officially. Zane needed to take care of something on shore."

"Well, I'll start with breakfast. Do you need me to bring anything back?"

"I'm good. I'll grab something after most of the passengers have disembarked."

The first people she ran into at the breakfast buffet were the Sassy Seniors. Today's shirt declared age was how many years of fun they'd had. Each woman wore a different number, all over one hundred.

"Sit with us, dear."

"Where is that hot man of yours?"

"Do you need to talk to us?"

"Did he forget to change his seasickness patch? I forgot on our trip to Antarctica." Linda shook her head as the others laughed.

"I don't think it's seasickness. I've never seen him like he was this morning." True. But the heat crawling up her cheeks wasn't going to help matters.

"Aw, he must have wanted you to be his nurse." Georgia's suggestive wink had the other women guffawing.

Elle's cheeks flamed. She stuffed eggs topped with salsa in her mouth and concentrated on a bite of the peppers.

"Are you going to go ashore?" asked Pat.

Elle ignored the comments about what she could do if she didn't. "Alan told me to go ahead on our excursion. If he takes anything, he'll be out for the next eight hours anyway."

The talk turned to her excursion to Antigua and theirs to Guatemala City. After breakfast, they went their separate ways.

With careful planning, Elle ended up in the disembarkation line two people in front of Cassie and Case. All was not well with that couple either.

"Can't you ditch them?" Case's question came out as a low growl.

"Only on the ship. They were part of the deal. Dad insisted. You agreed."

"I don't like them watching you."

Cassie laughed. "Why? Because they're big and handsome?"

Case grumbled something.

"They are so not into me. Think about it. They are sharing a tiny stateroom."

"So they are interested in me?"

"They'd better not be." Cassie's voice carried a tone of possessiveness. "Now, can we have fun today? I can't wait to see Antigua."

Elle bit her lip so she wouldn't laugh at the implication. Peter was definitely not interested in Case, and his partner was a happily married father of three. His wife was meeting him in Florida to take the reverse trip through the canal for their tenth anniversary. And they had separate staterooms. Elle made a note to let the

Texas bodyguards know about Cassie's lie about their romantic leanings in case they needed the cover. For some reason, she was feeling the need to justify having bodyguards. Sometimes principals, especially younger teens, did so before trying to evade their protectors.

The bus ride to Antiqua would take an hour and a half. Elle settled into her seat and texted Peter a warning. Then she sat back and texted Deidre. **Is Liam's firm still looking for females?**

—**Always**

I need to jump ship. She hadn't intended the pun but left it.

—**Alan?**

I lied when I said I was over him. If I survive the next eight days …

—**How soon do you want to start?**

March 15-ish. I'm planning on a week's vacation at my parents'. I may take a few days more. If Liam is willing to make me an offer, I'll turn in my two weeks' notice to Jethro today.

No message came through for a moment.

—**This is Liam. We would love to have you. But my wife is concerned you are making a bad choice.**

Married people. Of course Deidre had shared with him.

—**So sorry. Husband needs to keep mouth shut.**

Is that what you think?

—**I think you need to give Alan more time. During this assignment might not be the time to be honest about your feelings, but running away won't solve the problem.**

He's been clear. The only way I'm going to be able to finish this assignment is knowing that when I get off this ship in Miami, this is over.

—**Can I tell Liam about your college degree?**

If he is looking over your shoulder, you pretty much have. But if Dermot needs someone with those skills, I'm willing to work that side of the job too.

—**Does Alan know about your skills?**

Nope. Not unless he's googled me. And he's never mentioned it.

—Liam says you're hired at 10 percent more than you are making now. He may be grinning ear to ear about your computer skills. Push for 15 percent.

Elle bit her lip to keep from laughing and attracting any attention.

Can we work out the details when I'm in Florida? I have a feeling you may have overestimated my skills.

—Liam says fine. Still push for the fifteen.

Thanks. I'll give Jethro a verbal notice today.

—Wait until you're in Florida. It's still almost two weeks, and you don't need to add to the drama right now. It will make the job harder if Alan figures out you're leaving because of him.

She had a point. Alan's acting skills were only so-so. I'll wait. That way I can get things from Dermot in writing.

—Liam says he'll get an offer written up and send it to your personal email.

We land March 2. I won't be able to respond until then.

—Liam says perfect.

Thanks.

—As far as the assignment—you can do this.

Elle leaned back and watched the scenery. Her phone pinged again. Deidre added a final word.

—Alan is a good guy. Before you turn in your resignation, have an honest talk with him. He's the type who needs things laid out in black and white. You may think you've put your heart on the line, but he may have missed it. I don't want you to make the same mistake I almost made.

Elle closed her eyes to push down the emotions she didn't want to feel. Thanks, friend. :)

Alan dug through his bag to find the USB drive. He'd debated about not even watching whatever Mom had put on the USB. All night, he'd pondered what Dad had said about ZoElle reporting her attack. At one in the morning, he'd googled the process of reporting a rape. For the next two hours, he'd read news reports and blogs. He'd punched his pillows. The room had grown too hot as he tossed and turned. Sleeping in hadn't been his plan, but it had worked to avoid a conversation with ZoElle this morning. Asking the question running through his mind wouldn't do anything to help their tenuous relationship.

If Mom had gone to the trouble of making the video, there was a good reason for it. Better to watch it now. Then he'd have several hours of gym time to work out his frustrations with the court system and men who needed to be punched out at a minimum.

Mom's face filled the screen. "Alan, I've been concerned over the last few months, especially with your reaction to Elle's test results. I'd give you another lecture on life not being black and white, but that isn't going to work. Everything I am sharing with you can either be found online or in our files. Although, if you go looking for her files, I've locked them with my personal code.

"Our story starts two Octobers ago in Wisconsin. It's a beautiful Tuesday morning. Elle is in her third week of managing a new team, and their project hits a snag. *Yes, I am embellishing for your own good. Not everything is fact.* As she analyzed the new code, it becomes clear that someone sabotaged her project. Is it one of her new team members or another coworker who's jealous about her recent promotion? It's unusual to have a twenty-five-year-old team manager in her field, even if she is a UIUC grad."

What? He'd deliberately avoided digging into ZoElle's background to give her privacy. Alan paused the video and searched the alumni website of his alma mater, the University of Illinois at Urbana-Champaign. ZoElle Watson's name appeared. He did the math. She'd graduated with a master's degree in computer science at age twenty. He'd been twenty-two when he completed his bachelor's. A master's? Alan winced. He'd assumed she'd been a secretary from the way she'd talked about her old boss, her attacker, who was a programming manager. ZoElle never mentioned him in casual conversation. If she'd been managing a team, why had she left the field?

The smile she'd given him when he discussed the Hastings system hadn't been glazed-over disinterest; she'd been laughing at his attempting to put things in layman's terms. He'd assumed... *Charles Babbage!* She probably knew more than he did. ZoElle would even understand why he'd used *Babbage* as his go-to frustration word. No wonder she'd never asked him about the inventor of the computer.

Alan unpaused the video.

"Elle stayed late cleaning up the project so it would be ready to present to the VP the next day. A bit after ten, she went to her car, only to have it not start. Police later discovered someone had removed her spark plugs. A coworker, Nicholas Gooding, offered her a ride home. At the time, Elle lived in the house where she grew up." A photo of the house Alan had found ZoElle in filled the screen. "Her parents had moved to Florida for the winter on the first of September leaving her the house."

"Shortly after midnight, Elle dialed 911. Her unintelligible call was dropped. A second call came in five minutes later. ER doctors later confirmed she'd suffered a concussion. From the blood, investigators concluded she'd hit her head on the coffee table while fighting with her attacker. A friend picked Elle up from the hospital at about 10:00 a.m. on Wednesday. With her concussion, she'd called in sick to work. A team member made the presentation, incidentally failing to give Elle the credit she deserved."

Once again, his mother's face filled the screen. "I've debated showing you photos from that night. This is the only photo from the police report I decided I will show you."

It wasn't Elle but the mug shot of her forty-five-year-old attacker. He had scratches down his cheeks and a split lip.

"Thursday after phone conversations with HR and the VP, Elle worked from home. Friday morning, she was ready to leave the house for work when the first reporter showed up. Believing it was her friend, she answered the knock at her front door. I don't need to tell you how the rest of the day went when the media played the game of "that name sounds close enough." Early that afternoon, you arrived and whisked her away to Chicago."

Alan's mind filled in the details of those last few hours—ones he previously hadn't thought much about. He first saw her through the window, as sitting on the floor between the bar and the counter, arms around her knees like a scared child. It had taken him several tries to get her to talk with him. Once she'd confirmed his identity, a ridiculously long process requiring him to slip his driver's license through the doggy door before she let him in the Wisconsin house, she'd been composed not panicked. Only a few dried-up tear tracks remained. He'd only seen her defeated for a few seconds, yet ZoElle curled up on the floor was the picture he'd kept tucked in his mind.

Returning to Chicago, he'd planned to use his parents' home as a safe house for her. The safest house in the world was probably the house he'd grown up in, but his parents were out of town. In the end, he'd put her in the overly monitored Ogilvie Tower apartment his sister had used for her last Hastings assignment. She'd be safe given the building's security and the hidden cameras and microphones all over the apartment. His plan was to monitor the apartment via computer and stay far away. He'd rotate someone, preferably Deidre, out of another position to be with her. That plan had lasted until he'd returned with dinner and a few groceries and found ZoElle in the kitchen, holding a marble rolling pin above her head, ready to strike.

He'd forgotten to call out as he entered the apartment. Alan had taken the rolling pin from her, and she had thrown herself at him and started crying—messy-makeup-left-all-over-his-shirt crying. ZoElle hadn't cried the entire trip down.

Of all the images he remembered of that day, it should be the rolling-pin one. That ZoElle—strong, determined.

The video continued, showing a poised ZoElle on a national talk show only a week after the media storm had broken. The moderator explained the situation. A temp at the police station had scored $5,000 by selling information to a second-rate gossip blog after seeing photos of Nick Gooding and Zoe Wilson on a date in NYC and recognizing the names from a report she'd typed. The fact that Nicholas D. Gooding was fifteen years older and ZoElle Watson wasn't named Zoe had been buried under the sensational headlines. Nick and all his billions couldn't squash them fast enough. ZoElle had been caught in the crossfire, accused of everything from attempting to get Nick to pay her off to faking the rape report. Nick's investigators had found ZoElle, and the billionaire had wasted no time attempting to set things right. His personal phone call to Hastings Security was what pulled Alan out from behind his desk to personally deal with a client for the first time in months.

More recent interviews played, including the question-and-answer his father had spoken of.

Interviewer: "What was the most difficult moment of your experience?"

ZoElle. "That is a toss-up. The moment I realized my attacker wanted to murder me was life changing but not the hardest. The most difficult was probably my friend calling me the Friday after being attacked and not believing I wasn't behind the media storm. She said some nasty things, and I lost it."

Interviewer: "When did you know you would survive?"

ZoElle: "Before the media mess, I thought I could when my attacker was arrested. But then the entire world knew a partial truth, and I was painted as something I wasn't. I was getting hate posts on my social media, and I thought my life would never be normal. I was sitting in my kitchen, hiding and wishing my attacker had killed me, when someone knocked on my back door. I didn't realize it then, but he was an angel in disguise. Later, I tried to hit him over the head with a marble rolling pin. Realizing

I still wanted to fight and to live, even if there was absolutely no way I could win, was a turning point."

Interviewer: "You help teach self-defense classes. What advice do you give other women?"

ZoElle: "Report the attack. It's a choice. The more choices you can make to benefit you, the better life gets. Choosing to go on national TV was hard, but the experience gave me something back—my voice. Within hours, the public's opinion of ZoElle changed. For me, returning to my old job wasn't a good choice because my attacker was a coworker, and even after his conviction, it would have made for a nasty environment. Choosing to change careers wasn't running away. I made a choice to develop skills I hadn't had before. I found a career I love."

Interviewer: "So, you think life is all about choices?"

ZoElle: "No. Bad stuff happens. Life steals opportunities from you. Doors are closed. It's the choices you make after those things happen. I could have continued on in my old career and worked from home, ordered groceries online, and become a hermit. But my attacker would have won. This is *my* life, and I will not allow anyone else to control it."

The video ended.

Alan stared at the blank screen, trying to process what he'd seen. If he were a computer, he could fix the buffer overrun going on in his brain. He could shut down part of the system, relocate memory. What could he do with this? The fifteen seconds of memory he'd been clinging to were inaccurate.

Fifteen miles later, on the second treadmill to the left, Alan still didn't know how to reboot his brain. ZoElle had needed help, but she wasn't helpless. ZoElle had never been broken. He didn't have a place to shelve that fact. Worse, he had no idea how to apologize because every way he played the scenario, it ended in a passionate kiss.

And they were on assignment.

Not even the romance novel of one of her favorite authors could hold Elle's interest. She scrolled through the cruise app. "They have a showing of a new movie in the small theater in a half hour. Do you want to go?"

Alan looked up from his computer. "What are Cassie and Case doing?"

"Cassie has a sunburn. She wants to stay in tonight."

"How was the job today?" He closed his laptop.

"Nothing suspicious. A bit crowded, as expected." It had been odd being on her own.

"Sure, let's go to the movie. We need to wear our one-week-anniversary shirts anyway."

"I thought you were against ever wearing the shirt."

Alan put the laptop in the drawer. "Abbie has texted several times. The path of least resistance is to send her a photo of us in them."

Elle grabbed her shirt out of the closet and changed in the bathroom. When she came out, Alan was already in his. "Why do I have this urge to find our Sassy Seniors and take a group selfie?"

"Maybe it's the glittery ship embroidered under 'Cruisin' through our first week?'"

"My sister had too much fun with our assignment." Alan held the door open for her. "I think the triplets are making her a bit stir-crazy."

"Alex said she likes to tease you because you're so grumpy."

On the way to the theater, they snapped a couple of selfies. Alan picked up a tub of popcorn. The movie wasn't good—not that Elle paid attention after the popcorn ran out, because Alan reached over and held her hand.

IT WAS ALWAYS EASIER TO figure out what to say to ZoElle when she wasn't nearby. After the movie, they walked the decks discussing random things. Holding hands not because he had to but because he wanted to. Could she feel the difference? Frankly, the best part of the movie had been the excuse to hold her hand. Every time he tried to say something to that effect, a random fact about a star, the Panama Canal, or ship buoyancy came out of his mouth.

Now alone in the king-sized bed, he found that the words came, only to disappear as fast.

Alan reached for his phone. 3:42 a.m.

They had a week of the cruise left. Admitting he had feelings he'd like to explore while sharing a honeymoon suite could be disastrous. If she rejected him, the awkwardness would only increase. If she felt the same way, they'd have to agree not to pursue anything this week. He was already having a hard enough time not holding her hand or touching her when she was near. And then there was the whole losing-focus-on-the-client issue.

He could apologize for being a jerk and underestimating her after her test in January. Maybe that would get the friendship back on track. Then maybe he could sleep.

Another day at sea—their last before entering the canal. And the halfway point of the job. Elle stared out at the waves sparkling under the afternoon sun. Alan had gone to the gym for a second workout. He'd left halfway through their morning workout, pointing to his phone. She'd assumed it was something work-related. When she returned to their suite, he had showered and dressed. They'd gone to breakfast together but at the restaurant, not the buffet. Alan talked to every passenger at the table except for her—unless asking to pass the salt counted.

Elle closed the reading app. The Regency romance had lost its appeal. Who wanted to read about a brooding hero when they were living with one? Alan was going to change all her opinions on Mr. Darcy being the romantic, brooding type.

What had she done to earn the silent treatment this morning? He'd been chatty enough last night. And holding her hand. Weird. There wasn't a logical reason to hold her hand during the movie. No one had sat next to them. And the theater was half empty. Others must have known the movie wasn't worth the time. Had he figured out she was going to leave Hastings?

Deidre wouldn't have told him. Elle checked her phone. She'd sent the texts through her private messaging system, not the Hastings app. Her contract allowed Hastings Security to monitor her location while on duty for her safety, but her texting should be private.

When he came back, she'd have to ask him what was wrong. A message came through the app.

—C&C private poolside. Need eyes. Ship camera down.
 Be up in a minute.

Alan came in the door as Elle, now in swimsuit and cover-up, was ready to leave. "I'll hurry."

Elle frowned at his back and waited. She tugged at the strap on her top. The two-piece was a mistake. Putting it on to make Alan talk to her was a bad idea. Abbie had assured her the suit would make any man's jaw drop while still having more fabric than the average bikini. The problem was that Elle wasn't comfortable in the average one-piece. Even they showed too much skin. She should hurry and change.

Alan came out of the bedroom in a T-shirt, long trunks, and flip-flops. His skin still glistened from his work out. "Let's hurry."

No time to change.

They found Case and Cassie in the private pool for the passengers with exclusive club access—one perk of the suites they were staying in.

Elle sat down on a lounger near the pool. Alan sat down next to her. They both avoided looking directly at Case and Cassie, whose embrace would be more appropriate for a more private location.

"I need to rinse off." Alan dove into the far end of the pool, still wearing his T-shirt as usual.

Elle used his absence to arrange her cover-up in a causal way to keep herself as covered as possible. There was no hiding the fact that she wasn't wearing one of her modest one-pieces, but she could keep her midriff covered.

Case and Cassie came up for air when Alan left the pool.

"Elle, aren't you going to join us?" asked Cassie.

"No, I'll work on my tan."

Case's gaze raked over her. "Y'all will tan better without the cover-up."

Alan raised his brows as if noticing the outline of her suit under the lacy cover-up for the first time. He turned away.

"I'll burn better too." Elle lifted her book in a salute. As much as she wanted to, she couldn't be upset with Abbie for the suit recommendation. If this were a real honeymoon, and if she were alone with her new husband, it would have been more than appropriate. Eventually, Cassie and Case exited the pool, and Cassie sat down on the lounger on the other side of Elle. Case grabbed a towel and asked if anyone wanted drinks. Elle held up her water bottle, indicating she was fine.

"How is yesterday's sunburn? I'm surprised you're out here."

Cassie poured lotion on her legs. "You know husbands. Case really wanted to see me in this swimming suit, and I couldn't deny him. I think I've used half a bottle of lotion already." Her suit was the quintessential itsy-bitsy polka-dot bikini.

"Do you have a cover-up?"

"Case doesn't like me to wear one." Cassie's voice was barely above a whisper.

"Well, it's better than getting a sunburn."

Cassie's eyes darted to Case, who was returning with their drinks. "Are you going dancing tonight?"

"Alan? Did you want to go dancing tonight?"

He sat up, the front of his shirt already dry from the sun's rays. "Not sure. Did you want to go together?"

Case handed Cassie her iced tea.

"I said no alcohol." Cassie set her drink down on a small table between her and Elle.

"Sorry, babe." Case picked up the drink and stumbled, both his drink and Cassie's raining down on Elle.

Instinctively, she jumped out of her seat. The liquid had doused her hair and was dripping down her face. She tried not to gag at the stench of alcohol. The lacy cover-up clung to her, hiding nothing.

"Nice suit," smirked Case.

Cassie handed Elle a towel. "Jump in the pool and rinse off. I'm sure it's seen worse."

Not looking in Alan's direction, Elle struggled out of the cover-up, jumped in the pool, and dove to the bottom. The jerk. If Cassie weren't already married to him, Elle would warn her off. What did she see in him?

She swam the short length of the pool, wishing it were longer. Twenty or so laps wouldn't even start to lessen the tension flowing through her. Case's eyes never left her body. Elle vowed to throw the suit away. Cassie pointed Case back to the bar, and Elle escaped while his back was turned.

Alan met her at the end of the pool with two towels. Elle quickly wrapped one around herself. "You okay?"

"Mostly." She dried off quickly, keeping Alan between her and Case.

"Would you like my shirt?" He didn't wait for an answer before pulling it off over his head.

"Thanks." His smelled like a warm hug.

Alan wrapped an arm around her waist. "You sure you're okay?" His words tickled her ear.

"Nothing like a good alcohol-and-ice bath to liven up your day. They say a beer rinse is good for your hair."

On the other side of the pool, Cassie gathered her things. She set off for the rooms with Case running after her.

"Sorry I didn't step in. I didn't realize he'd already been drinking."

"Looks like our job is done here." Elle gathered her book and sunglasses. The sopping book would go the same place her swimsuit would. "I hope his stunt didn't start too big of a fight. I'd hate to have Cassie hurt on my account."

"What about you being hurt?" Concern laced his voice. He was back in protector mode.

"I'm a bodyguard, and according to your mom, I'm not going to die of embarrassment."

Alan handed her another towel. "If I was the hero in one of your historical romances, I would call him out and meet him at dawn."

"What do you know about my romances?"

"I've lost several bets with Abbie over the years. I think I've seen every single Jane Austen movie there is."

"How did I not know this?"

"As you said the other day, you don't know everything about me." Alan laughed.

But she'd like to.

—Cassie and Case in casino. We will cover. PS. Your mom is winning again.

Alan showed ZoElle the message. "Looks like we have another evening free."

"We could play a game."

"All we have is two decks of cards."

"We have two laptops. I'm sure I can keep up with you in some of your computer games."

"You're a gamer?" After last night's revelation about her degree, he shouldn't be surprised.

ZoElle laughed. "Don't look so shocked. If you can watch period romances, I can play *League of Legends*—only I don't have my laptop."

"They have an Xbox lounge. We could go check it out."

ZoElle tapped her chin. "On one condition."

"As long as it doesn't involve watching men ride horses while wearing suits and women swooning."

"Is that all you got out of Jane Austen?"

"No. I learned that playing the piano is an essential part of catching a mate." Alan jumped back when ZoElle swatted at him.

"Lucky for you, my condition had nothing to do with Regency romance. Remember last spring when I first flipped you on your back and you got so annoyed?"

"I was surprised." And a bit bruised.

"Promise me you'll be less grouchy when I trounce you." Her teasing grin was begging for retaliation.

"Trounce me? We don't even know what game we're playing yet."

ZoElle ducked under his arm and opened the cabin door. "It won't matter."

"Those sound like fighting words."

ZoElle pushed the button for the elevator. "Someone sounds nervous. Scared of losing to a girl?"

"I've lost to girls before." There was one particular woman in his favorite game that almost always bested him. elZ15. At least he was pretty sure she was a woman.

The Xbox lounge wasn't as empty as Alan assumed it would be, but they were able to get a screen to themselves. Alan input his gamer name, lilRok85.

"Little Rock?"

"It's what Alan means in Celtic. I had to write an origin-of-my-name paper in seventh grade. I thought it was a cool name."

"I wasn't questioning the origin." ZoElle bit her lip. "More like your identity."

ZoElle typed in her screen name: elZ15.

"Wait a minute. We've been battling for years."

"You mean you've been losing for years. Ready to lose again?"

Alan saluted the screen with his controller. "It's on." Because no matter the score of the game, knowing ZoElle was elZ15 was the biggest win ever.

For the past couple of months, she'd suspected Alan could be lilRok85, but she'd avoided getting to know her fellow players on a personal level after a bad experience her junior year of college. Adam had called Alan "Little Rock" over the comms one night when Alan was being stubborn over something. The realization that they'd played each other for more than four years was mind-blowing—knowing someone and not knowing someone all at the same time.

LilRok was never rude in his gaming interactions—proof he was the same person off-line. Once, two, or three years ago, he even defended her when a foul-mouthed player had gone off on her after she had failed to defend his position.

They found a new game neither of them had played. The graphics were fine, but the game itself was lacking, coming across as a reboot of other games. At eleven they quit playing and called the game a draw. They both needed sleep for tomorrow's excursion into Costa Rica. Three teenage boys expressed their dismay at the couple ending the game as they handed off their controllers.

"I can't believe we've been online friends for so many years." Alan held her hand on the way back to their room.

"You've been good competition." Elle bit back a laugh. "You realize we played each other that first week we met. I remember you commenting on how recklessly I played."

Alan furrowed his brow. "I never realized. How did I miss that?"

"Supposedly, I was in bed sleeping and you were off duty. I couldn't sleep those first few weeks. Beating up men in games was a good release for me. There was a lot of silent yelling at the screen because I was afraid you would hear me and come rushing in, especially when we were in New York."

"That could have been interesting, especially if you'd just killed my character."

"Which I am sure I did multiple times. I was angry, and I wanted answers about why he tried to kill me and what his plan was. Was it just to warn me off, or were rape and murder part of it? Although he seemed shocked to learn I was alive, I didn't have one of those go-toward-the-light experiences, so I don't think I was anything other than unconscious."

"Did you ever get answers?"

"No. They might have come out in a trial or at least some version of them, but Nick spared me that. Not that he'll admit it, but I am sure he's the reason there was a guilty plea."

They entered their cabin. "Do you still have nightmares?"

"Occasionally, but I usually stop my dreams by using a move Deidre taught me or by fixing my car so he can't drive me home. My therapist taught me some techniques to control the dreams using real life skills. I took a basic auto mechanics course at the community college. Next time my car won't start, I'll know if someone's disabled it."

"Does it bother you to talk about this?" Alan sat down next to her on the couch.

"With you? No. Sometimes one of the interviewers tries to make the interview about the details. That annoys me because Zoe and I are trying to get the message about responsible media out, not fulfill some morbid curiosity. You never pushed or even asked."

"I had no clue what to say. I just knew I had to keep you safe."

"I still can't believe I almost hit you with the rolling pin." She'd learned since that her stance wouldn't have had the desired effect. Using the rolling pin in a baseball bat swing would have been more effective than the over-the-head move she'd tried. She didn't have enough force against a man as tall as Alan.

"It was my fault. I should have called out when I came in. Not enough field experience."

Elle covered her mouth and forced a yawn. She needed the conversation to end, and the logical end was a hug, and maybe her kissing him . . . or being rejected. Either option wasn't good. "I'll go brush my teeth, and then you can have the bathroom and bedroom."

For the first night of the cruise, Alan didn't argue about the sleeping arrangements. Maybe he sensed the conversation needed to end too.

FROM THE DOCK, COSTA RICA didn't look much different from the last place they stopped. Alan ran his hand down his face. Yesterday had been awkward in a million little ways. Knowing what he now knew, everything about ZoElle had changed. He checked his laundry drawer. She hadn't returned his shirt. Had she deliberately kept it? He smiled.

They needed to talk more. Last night's conversation had opened a door. Alan wanted to tell her what his mother had sent him. Of course, he followed up with his own research. He had found everything, including the mugshots of her attacker, with some pointed Web surfing. Something he'd never done with her background check, as it seemed too invasive. He'd gotten further into her history than he planned—the Junior Regional Ballroom Dance competition was adorably cute.

Alan checked the schedule and saw that they were on an excursion involving a long train ride. There would be time to talk. Cassie and Case would be with Peter and Zane at yet another orphanage. His parents were touring a nearby historical theater.

The line to their excursion was longer than Alan expected. Four voices caught ZoElle's attention, and she started chatting with their cruise friends. All he could think about was how there would be no private conversation with the Sassy Seniors sitting near them.

"Oh, how cute! You're wearing matching shirts today."

Not the silly T-shirts Abbie sent. They'd accidentally chosen the same color blue today.

"Smile!"

"Say cheese."

"Kiss her."

"Not the cheek."

"You're newlyweds! Act like it."

Alan lost track of how many times Elle pulled the blush-into-his-shirt move. She added lips-almost-touching, burst-into-giggles to the hide-her-face-in-the-chest move. In over four hours with the Sassy Seniors and their camera phones, Alan had avoided all but two kiss requests, which they both kept to brushing lips. The discussion on childbearing and timing of first children they couldn't avoid no matter how many times they changed the subject.

ZoElle's smile had yet to extend to her eyes and stiffened by the hour, as did his own.

When the excursion ended, they ducked into a tourist-trap store as the Sassy Seniors made a beeline for a café.

"They really are the most darling of people." ZoElle examined a wooden toucan.

"The conversation about which foods are best to eat to get a baby boy was somewhat interesting."

"I don't think eating a banana a day guarantees a boy."

"Abbie hates bananas." Alan checked the size on a toddler T-shirt. He did need to bring home souvenirs for all four nephews and his niece.

"And she has three boys." ZoElle turned her attention to the jewelry counter.

They returned to the ship early enough that there was no line.

"May I use your computer to send an email? I promised Mom an update, and I hate sending long ones from my phone."

"Sure. My mom and dad are back. I'm going to go talk with them for a few minutes."

They separated at the elevators. He heard raised voices from outside his parents' room. Mostly his mother's.

"What was he thinking?"

"That makes two of our boys."

Alan knocked on the door anyway. Jethro answered.

"I'm not sure what I did, but I can hear you in the hall." Alan stayed back from where his mother crossed the small room.

"It's not you. Andrew is married."

"What?"

"Yesterday, their plane had mechanical problems, and they were forced to land in Colorado on the way home at a small airport in Loveland. Apparently, Jordan thought it would be cute to buy a wedding gown in a city named Loveland. Somehow, finding the gown metamorphosed into a trip to the courthouse. They sent us pictures." Melanie shoved her tablet into Alan's hands, and there was Jordan in a white dress, kissing Andrew.

"They look happy." Alan handed the tablet back.

"They look married." Melanie sat down in the single chair.

Jethro sat on the bed. "They're smirking because the paparazzi missed the entire thing."

"Considering Jordan's last several months, I can see why they did it that way. The media hasn't given them a break since Andrew proposed."

"Never propose in public." Melanie waved a finger at Alan. "And don't you dare get married without inviting me to the wedding. Two sons got married without me."

"Alex and Kimberly had a formal renewal of their vows. It wasn't like they intended to stay married the first time." Although he had originally been annoyed with Alex, he'd defended his brother. Alex had made a hard choice in order to save his client. Kimberly's soft voice made her his favorite sister-in-law—that and her drawings of him as a platypus. She'd chosen the platypus because it was cute, unique, and venomous, implying that Alan didn't look as dangerous as he could be.

"But Andrew and Jordan aren't going to have any type of ceremony for anyone."

Jethro shook his head. "Do you really think Claire Lee is going to skip hosting at least one party?"

"It won't be the same."

"Mom, are you sad they got married without you or that you didn't get to meet Kevin Bacon?" Jordan's famous grandmother, Claire, had been threatening to invite Kevin to the wedding for months.

Melanie laughed. "You are right. It's more the shock. Did you need to talk about something?"

Now was not the time to get advice about his relationship with ZoElle. Mom would have him proposing before dinner. "No, I should get back to our stateroom."

Hopefully ZoElle's reaction to Andrew's marriage would be better. Unfortunately, he opened the door to be greeted by another yell.

"Why? Why now?" ZoElle sat at the table, staring at his computer screen.

"Why what?"

She turned the computer to face him. A dozen browser tabs remained open from his search on ZoElle Watson. Dance competitions, computer-science awards, the coverage of her attacker's guilty plea. Pretty much her entire life. He'd cyberstalked her.

"After a year and a half, you would ask Google before asking me?" She blinked back a tear. "At least I know why you've been acting so weird." She stood and walked to the door. "Text me when you need me to play the dutiful newlywed. Until then, I need some space."

Alan closed his browser. Mom didn't need to worry about his marriage anytime soon.

Elle checked with the assistant security crew chief. An hour and a half remained before the passengers had to reboard—more than enough time to consume some Costa Rican chocolate. She made her way to the shops near the wharf that catered to cruise passengers. A woman in a floppy hat hurried in her direction, nearly bumping into Elle.

"Cassie?"

"Oh, sorry." Tears trailed down the heiress's cheeks.

Elle looked around for Peter or Zane. A shadow of a man not built like either of them ducked into an alley. "Where's Case?"

"He got mad at me, then took a punch at Peter. The café owner wasn't happy and called the police. I slipped out as soon as everyone started recording things on their phones. I was going to the ship. Where's Alan?"

The man still stood in the shadows of the alley, watching them.

"We had an argument. I decided to shop for the famous chocolate I've heard about. Want to join me?" Elle twisted her earring to start broadcasting, not knowing how well anyone would pick up the signal from the ship or if Peter and Zane even could.

Cassie bit her lip. "I probably shouldn't, but I am so tired of doing what everyone tells me to. Look out, chocolate, here we come."

As Elle led Cassie back up the wharf and past the man lurking in the shadows, he moved deeper into the alley.

"*Cielo de Chocolate.* Cassie, this shop might have something good enough to help us forget our husband issues." Her words should be enough to alert the Hastings or someone to their location if the tracker wasn't being accurate.

Elle recognized another passenger from the ship as she hovered between chocolate choices and kept an eye out. Minutes later, Jethro and Melanie came in, Melanie cooling herself with a bright-red fan she'd picked up on the excursion two days ago. "I need chocolate."

Jethro laughed loudly. "Whatever you say, dear."

Melanie joined Cassie and Elle at the counter. "I'd ask where your husbands are, but it took mine years to understand my need for chocolate."

They spent several minutes choosing the best chocolates. Jethro came to stand behind his wife. "We should get back to the ship. We don't want to be caught in those long lines."

Cassie checked her phone. "That sounds like a good idea."

Once on the ship, Elle convinced Cassie to hang out in the private lounge until Case returned with the bodyguards. Alan followed behind. No one had any bruises. Peter looked ready to give Cassie the stay-with-your-bodyguard lecture. Elle shook her head and mouthed "Later."

Peter raised a brow and stepped back. Cassie and Case went to their stateroom. Elle held up her phone. "Give me five minutes and I'll debrief."

Alan followed her into their stateroom. "I'm really—"

Elle whirled around. "Alan, not now. I need to focus. Cassie was being followed. Whatever reason you have for betraying my friendship comes second to our clients' safety."

Trying to ignore the shock on his face, Elle sat on the couch and opened the Hastings app for a conference call. Alan sat on the chair opposite.

Elle started the call with Jethro, Melanie, Peter, and Zane. "There was a man following her, but I didn't get a good look at him. Six one, six two. Lean. I don't think he was Costa Rican. Sorry. I wish I'd gotten a better look. I mostly wanted to get Cassie off the street."

"Kudos on the alert you sent. Jethro and I found you without any problems," said Melanie.

Peter ran a hand through his hair. "I still don't understand why Case tried to punch me. He wasn't as drunk as he was acting."

"He can't stand you because you're single and Cassie listens to you," said his partner.

"So, what is the plan for the two days in Columbia?" asked Elle. "Is she doing more orphanages?"

"Not if Case has his way. We have two days on ship before Columbia, so anything can change. I'm glad this ship doesn't stop in the canal," said Peter.

"What if we split them up? I can tell her I'd love to see the orphanages, and Alan and Case can do a guy's day." Elle mentioned the first plan she could think of.

"It might work. At the very least it gets you on-site with her. She doesn't know you're more than a secretary, does she?"

"No, I mentioned I'd taken some self-defense classes, but Case just snorted. He doesn't think I'm a threat."

"Elle is the best-kept secret we have," said Jethro.

"We have two days to convince Cassie to take you along," said Zane.

"No problem. My new enthusiasm for orphanages will get me an invitation." Elle ended the call.

Alan ran his hands through his hair. "May I apologize now?"

"I only wish you would have asked me instead of searching the web."

"Would you have told me anything I wanted to know?"

"We're friends. Of course I would have."

"Then why didn't you tell me you were a programmer? A master's. I can't believe you let me teach you about the Hastings app and how to do the scheduling. Were you laughing the entire time? Not that it makes my snooping any better, but friends don't lie to friends."

Elle looked up at the ceiling. "When you rescued me, you knew where I worked. You assumed I was an office assistant. I liked the anonymity your assumption gave me. I wasn't Math Girl or the female programmer. The night he almost killed me, he made sure I knew it was because I was a woman doing a man's work. He told me he didn't think I knew I was a woman and a lot of other things. Somehow, being an office assistant like every other female on the planet seemed like such a lovely job. I know that's totally not feminist, politically correct, or anything else. I was dealing with a lot of trauma, and I needed to be the same as everyone else."

"Anyway, when I relocated to Chicago, I could be one of many. Nick offered to help me get a job at C&O with Colin. I told him I wasn't ready to return to programming, and there was an opening at Hastings for a receptionist. But once I saw Deidre in action, I knew I wanted to be a bodyguard. Ironically, I changed one female minority job for another. There was something so freeing about it. Yes, I was one of the women, but no one dared insult me to my face about being a bodyguard. And I felt valued as there are times being female makes me more valuable than all the ex-seals in the business."

Alan leaned forward. "That explains why you mopped up everything like a sponge. I never did tell you how ingenious I thought the zipper-bag thing with Kimberly's letter was."

"You didn't, but I didn't expect you to either." Elle shrugged and pretended to take great interest in the throw pillow.

"Who knew about your degree?"

"Other than Jethro and Melanie? Colin Ogilvie and Diedre."

"How did he know?"

"I made a mistake last September. I was part of his detail on a trip to Seattle. He was frustrated with some program he was working on. We were sitting next to each other in the back of an SUV. I looked at the code and told him to reverse the order of some lines." Elle shrugged. "It worked. It took him a day to realize what I'd done. You know how he gets when he's solving a problem."

Alan laughed. "His detail's primary purpose is to keep him from walking into walls and busy streets."

"Anyway, he asked how I knew the solution and offered me a job."

"You didn't take it?"

"No, I'd come off Kimberly's detail, and I didn't want to return to a life behind a bunch of monitors. But I have done a couple of contract jobs for him."

"Like what?"

"You know the Hastings-app upgrade?"

Alan covered his eyes with one hand. "You're telling me I made you pass off training on something you designed?"

"Yup."

"But you got an answer wrong."

"No, you asked the wrong question. And now you know why I didn't tell you."

"I would have been embarrassed?"

"It would have hurt you." It hadn't been the only reason, but hurting him was a big one. She also didn't want Alan trying to keep her behind a computer in the office.

Alan stood and walked around the table. "I'm not sure how to take that."

"I didn't want you to look at me as anything other than Elle the bodyguard or wonder if I wanted to take your job. You do your job better than anyone else, which doesn't actually entail any programming..."

"Would you have ever told me?"

"Probably."

Her phone beeped. "Cassie and Case are headed to dinner and the casino. We need to get moving."

Elle stood. Alan laid his hand on her arm. "Where does this leave us?"

"Two coworkers doing a job."

THE UNCOMFORTABLE SILENCE THAT FILLED the suite since last night grew as the day progressed. Alan checked the ship's itinerary again. A full day at sea and a day through the canal. ZoElle had retreated to the deck with a book she'd purchased in one of the shops after breakfast—the thick biography of a politician.

The fear of wandering the deck alone and getting caught by the Sassy Seniors kept Alan sitting at the table and staring at a computer game that wasn't any fun without elZ15.

Enough.

Alan closed his laptop and went out to the deck.

"We need to talk."

ZoElle closed her book. "No, we don't. It will only end up being excuses and explanations. We've made it ten days. We've both—"

Voices on the other side of the privacy wall interrupted them.

"Babe, I promise, no more drinking."

Both Alan and ZoElle strained to hear Cassie's muffled reply. ZoElle shook her head and frowned.

"It's just that I can't drink when I am on call."

"You told me on New Year's Eve you only drank on special occasions."

"Our honeymoon is a special occasion ..." The pronounced drawl indicated that Case had already had enough to drink for the day.

"I'm serious, Case. No more drinking."

"Hey! Where are you going?"

ZoElle hopped up from the lounge chair, then hurried through their stateroom and out the door. Case yelled again and went into his stateroom. He came out a moment later muttering profanities about his wife running off.

Alan tapped a message into the app. **C & C fighting. ZoElle is with Cassie. Case is drunk again.**

Jogging, Elle caught up with the elevator before the doors shut. Cassie's shoulders were slumped. Another person and a crew member stood in the elevator with them.

"I've chipped off most of my polish from last week. Do you want to go see when the next spa appointments are?" Elle hoped her question would give Cassie a reason to include her in wherever she was going.

Cassie studied her own nails. "That's a good idea." She pushed the button for the spa deck.

Elle followed her off. The crew member exited behind them, then turned the other direction. Odd. She hadn't seen crew members on the passenger elevators since boarding, when they were being escorted to their suites. There weren't any mani-pedi appointments available until the following day. Cassie and Elle booked them, then found a quiet table in one of the lounges.

"Is something wrong?"

Cassie shook her head and looked at the window. After a moment, she turned back. "Did you hear us fighting?"

"Yes, I did. I figured you might need a friend."

"I don't understand what's up with his drinking. I think he drank today just to annoy me."

"Did he drink at all while you dated?"

"Just one drink on New Year's. He didn't even have the spiked punch at the hospital holiday party. Until this cruise, I would have said he was dry. I just don't get it. I don't like the drunk Case."

"To be honest, I don't either."

"I am so sorry about what he did at the pool the other day."

"It wasn't your fault." Elle spotted one of the ship's cameras over Cassie's shoulder. Someone would know where Cassie was by now.

"I know. I just hope when we get back to Dallas and he starts at the hospital, things go back to the way they were."

"You could ask the room steward to not stock your minibar. Alan and I told her we don't drink, so we only have soda in ours."

"That's a good idea. Case won't be happy. I know it's stupid to sound so insecure. It's just that I am. Every guy figures out how many zeros are in my name, and that's all they can think about. It tends to make a woman second-guess herself when the guy takes off the moment he sees the prenup. Granddad set out a doozy of one too. If he divorces me in under ten years, nothing. If I divorce him for almost any reason, he gets nothing. If I die, the money will be held for five years before he gets a penny." Cassie sucked in a breath. "I can't tell you how many boyfriends have literally run from me upon hearing the terms."

Elle's heart went out to her. She'd had a few men ask her out for the wrong reasons, especially since her attack. There were those who were morbidly interested in that particular part of her life. "That would be upsetting."

"We just agree on so many things. His work in Africa aligns so well with my vision. I've also been looking to do more in Texas and other states. There are so many vulnerable children. Case even helped dismantle a child-trafficking ring."

"I can see why you are so disappointed with his drinking."

"What about you? Where's Alan?"

"We had a bit of a tiff ourselves."

"Maybe the ten-day fight, then."

Elle tipped her head. "Ten-day fight. I've never heard of it."

"I just made it up. What did you fight about? If I can ask."

"I asked to use Alan's computer, and his browser was open. Every tab was about me. I was upset because he didn't feel he could just ask me about my history."

"Did you ask him why he did it?"

Elle replayed the conversation. "I don't think I did. We got derailed on parts of my life I'd never told him—things that despite our knowing each other for a year and a half, he never knew."

"Were you deliberately hiding your past from him?"

An uneasy feeling churned inside Elle. She had gone out of her way not to be any more computer savvy than the next person in the office. "I was hiding my master's degree from everyone, but since he is Hastings's computer tech wizard, I think he took the truth hard because I am a programmer and he explained a program I designed to me ..." She bit her lip. His discovery of that part of her past must have stung. "I think I hurt him. I didn't realize until now ..."

"That you could be part of the problem? This marriage thing is tricky, isn't it?" Cassie's laugh was lighter. Elle didn't know that she'd helped Cassie at all. She tried to focus on her friend, but her mind was working on ways to apologize to Alan. If she had a decent computer, she could ... Rats. She'd missed Cassie's comment.

"I said, 'Shall we go to lunch together?' They have that women's-only lunch buffet today with the comedian."

"That sounds fun."

It was dinnertime before Cassie and Elle returned to their suites. Cassie found their steward and ordered room service along with an emptying of the minibar. Giving in to peer pressure, Elle also ordered a special candlelight room-service meal.

Elle arrived back at the stateroom before the meal.

Alan sat at his computer. "How's Cassie?"

"Better. Was anyone else shadowing her?"

"Zane was up in ship security. He took me there today. It's rather mind-blowing—so many monitors and the stupid things people do, not realizing they're being watched. You two looked like you enjoyed lunch."

"It was nice to have some girl time. Did you talk with Case?"

"For a moment. He seemed to have sobered up. He went to talk to some crew member. They have AA meetings on the ship."

"I would have never thought about addiction meetings, but it makes sense. A fifteen-day cruise would be hard for someone used to weekly or semiweekly meetings."

Elle sat down across from Alan. "I owe you an apology for earlier. I blew up without even finding out why, after all this time, you investigated my background. Maybe we should start that conversation over."

He closed his laptop. "The short version is that Mom and Dad gave me a lecture about not everything being black and white, and they pointed out how I was pretty closed-minded when it came to you. That I'd been very unfair, especially in opposing your promotion. Mom gave me some facts, and I fell down a rabbit hole learning more about you—and in the process learned what a jerk I've been. I'm really sorry, especially for the promotion thing."

"What they say about first impressions must be true. That is the me you always see, isn't it?" Her first impression of Alan had been that he was an angel sent to save her…no wonder she had a crush bigger than the Pacific.

"Not anymore. I'm trying to remember you that night with the rolling pin, ready to fight me off."

"We both know I would have lost that fight, right?" ZoElle smiled.

"That isn't the point. You were willing to try, and after the week you had, that says so much about you. It even explains why you would give up programming to stand around and hope nothing happens all day."

A knock sounded on the door. Dinner was served.

Facts and stories about the Panama Canal came intermittently over the ship's loudspeakers and internal television systems. Alan leaned against the balcony railing and watched the ship slowly rise in the lock.

"If this was built today, I think it would have taken longer."

Alan turned to where ZoElle sat. "Why do you say that?"

"Red tape. Environmental studies. Stuff like that."

"You're probably right." Alan returned his attention to the lock. They'd cleared much of the air last night, at least enough to be on friendly terms again, though there was still that elephant on his side of the room. He couldn't risk their assignment by declaring his feelings. Maybe if they got through the next three days, he could on their last night at sea. The next two days in Colombia would be the most dangerous, with some low-level drug lord wanting to make a name for himself, or someone disgruntled that they'd been deported. Zane and Peter were more concerned about the next two stops. Mostly because other than the person ZoElle saw possibly following Cassie, nothing else had happened.

They'd all jumped a time or two the past eleven days when a male passenger or crew member had taken too much interest in Cassie. Yesterday in the command room, Alan had counted at least five men who seemed to be following Cassie and Elle. Zane was right about telling him to relax. As soon as they noticed Cassie's diamond, they backed off.

If Cassie did face a threat, it would be in the next two days. With no more port stops between Columbia and Miami, an attempt at sea was unlikely.

ZoElle joined him at the railing. "The ship's movement feels different in the canal. I wonder if you would still feel seasick here."

Alan touched the patch behind his ear. "I could take it off and find out."

She held up a hand and stepped back. "No, thank you. Let's keep this hypothetical."

"Do you realize how bad I'll get ribbed in the office when that becomes general knowledge?"

"Yes, I do, and having been on the receiving end, you'll deserve every bit of plastic barf they put on your keyboard."

"You sound like you're looking forward to it."

"I may have already told Deidre."

Alan lunged for her, not sure what he'd do if he caught her. Tickling her wasn't on the list of forbidden things. Kissing her? Well…

But ZoElle was too quick and locked the sliding glass door. Good thing he could get paybacks in just a couple more days.

THE ORPHANAGE WASN'T WHAT ELLE expected. The children clamored around them, cheering and smiling. Case pled a headache and didn't come, but none of the bodyguards minded.

Cassie and Elle rocked the babies and sang them songs. Cassie spoke with the director at length in rapid-fire Spanish. Though Elle struggled to follow what she was saying, Peter and Zane followed every word. The tour took only two hours with an extra hour for lunch.

After they left, Cassie asked them to find a quiet café where she typed into her phone for another hour.

Alan took a seat next to Peter. "Is this how it always goes?"

"If you take out Dr. Johnson's inappropriate remarks and trying to make out with his wife, yes."

Elle played with the straw in her drink. "I thought he worked for one of those third-world doctor charities."

"That is what his résumé says." Peter never took his eyes off Cassie.

"You don't like the doctor, do you?" asked Elle.

"Not for me to like or dislike. My job is to keep Cassie safe."

The unspoken censure lay hidden beneath Peter's tone. He was above caring too much for his client, unlike the Hastings Security siblings. Elle had seen the veiled comments about the permanent client-bodyguard relationships on several chat forums. The latest was that the Hastings were officially done since the only one left was married to his computer. That bothered Alan. Even if he had feelings for her beyond friendship, his reputation might keep him away. Elle promised Diedre she'd have a conversation with him. The last night of the cruise would be her chance. Once she stepped onto US soil, she wouldn't be working for the Hastings anymore. The third draft of her resignation sat ready to send in her phone.

They did a little sightseeing before returning to the ship early. Since Case wasn't in his and Cassie's room, Elle and Cassie chatted about a million little things in the lobby until dinner time.

After dinner, Melanie and Jethro took over the watch. Alan challenged her to an Xbox rematch, but the lounge was full, so they called it an early night. The 20,345 steps she'd accumulated during the day had served her well, and she fell asleep without difficulty.

The next day was nearly the same, only Case came along. There was enough tension in the air that even the brick walls could feel it. Abbie always teased Alan about not being perceptive. The orphanage visit was short and all business. ZoElle hugged and talked with the children, while Cassie only paid attention to the director. Peter and Zane stood at the edge of the room, leaving little doubt they were on duty. Alan stood near ZoElle, trying to keep his personal security instincts at bay and not join Peter and Zane.

By the time the orphanage tour ended, Alan found it difficult to find a single kind word for Case, quite sure he was witnessing the beginning of an abusive relationship. No wonder Peter found it difficult to watch Cassie. It was bad enough to be called in as personal security once a restraining order had been filed, another to watch it unfold. ZoElle managed to stay near Cassie's side despite Case's attempts to send ZoElle off.

The attempt on Cassie came at an upscale boutique Case insisted they visit. The prices were not outlandish by Chicago standards, but they were still above what ZoElle could easily spend on a dress. ZoElle accompanied Cassie to the changing area down a long dark hall. Peter frowned. Alan nodded in agreement. Changing areas were often near rear exits.

Alan followed the women. "Elle, do you need any help?"

Halfway down the hall, Case grabbed him by the shoulder. "You are not going near my wife while she is—"

Bang!

"Pervert!" ZoElle's yell had Alan running down the hall. An exterior door slammed shut.

ZoElle cradled Cassie in her arms. Her eye's met Alan's. "Just someone trying to get a peek through the curtains." The look in her eyes told him there was more to the story.

Alan opened the door to the alley. No one was in sight. By the time he returned to the dressing room, Cassie was speaking quietly to Case. "He didn't see anything. I hadn't even taken off my shirt."

ZoElle gathered the dresses. "I don't feel like trying anything on."

"But that yellow one is so cute."

"Only because it matches your blue one." ZoElle laughed as she expertly herded Cassie back to the front of the store, where Cassie spoke with the saleswoman in rapid Spanish before they left the store and returned to the ship.

Once they were alone in their stateroom, ZoElle sent a message, calling for another meeting. Alan sat down on the opposite end of the couch, waiting for her to tell him what happened.

"I cleared the first dressing room and put Cassie in there so I would be between her and the alley, then I checked the other room and put my dress on the hook. I was clearing the rest of the hallway, and he was just there, standing in the doorway."

Peter ran a hand through his hair. "I should have checked the rooms before she went in."

"You knew I would." ZoElle waved his comment away. "But then you wouldn't have known that I am pretty sure he's the same man I saw in Costa Rica."

Elle waited for the shock to go through the group. "Same build and tanned skin, from what I could see. He had a ski mask on. My scream got rid of him, so I didn't need to blow my cover. He was too far away to grab."

"The same man in Costa Rica and Columbia?" asked Melanie.

"He also had on a nice watch, like an Apple Watch but chunkier. I think I've seen that watch before on this cruise, but I can't place it. There could be dozens of them." Elle pinched her eyes closed, trying to visualize the man in Costa Rica. He'd been wearing a watch, but she hadn't gotten a good look at it.

Jethro rubbed his chin. "Are you sure it's the same man?"

Elle closed her eyes again and tried to picture them side by side. "My first thought was that he was the same person. Since I didn't get a good look at him either time, I'd put the match around 70 percent. Mostly his build. But it would be like seeing all the Hastings brothers in the dark if you didn't know them well. They all look similar."

Alan laughed along with his parents.

"Elle, if you saw the watch again, could you identify it?" asked Peter.

"Probably."

"Six foot, lean, tan." Zane ticked off the known facts. "I'll work on filtering the passengers on the security video and see if we come up with any matches. It's too coincidental."

No one needed to say how much they didn't like coincidences.

The conference call ended.

Elle went into the bathroom for a little privacy. Only two more days of having to be near Alan. Unfortunately, they would both be at sea. Unless Zane found someone suspicious, there would be little to do other than show up wherever Cassie was.

Tomorrow night would be the last formal night. Dancing and dinner. If not for this assignment, she could have gone her entire life without knowing that Alan knew how to dance, which was almost as bad as knowing what his kisses were like. She needed to convince Melanie to take the Saturday-night watch and switch rooms with Alan. If the talk went poorly, they wouldn't be able to be in the same room. If it went well, Alan's sense of propriety wouldn't let them stay in the same room. To be honest, her' wouldn't either.

Elle turned on the shower and let the tears run down her cheeks. If her wish were to be like the rest of the females in the world, that wish was granted. She couldn't give a single good reason for her tears other than crying over a man. And according to every chick-flick ever made, a man was the number one reason women cried.

Case and Cassie had ordered room service.

Alan ran his hand through his hair, not sure whether the news was welcome or not. With only two days left of the job, he couldn't afford to do anything other than focus on Cassie's safety. As soon as Cassie was safely off the ship and under Peter's care, he'd finish the kiss he'd started in the captain's quarters and beg ZoElle to give him a chance.

Five days of pondering on the situation was more than enough for him to realize what an idiot he'd been.

He needed to reboot the relationship.

ZoElle came out of the bathroom in a pair of sweats and her hair wrapped in a towel. "Do we need to put on an appearance tonight?"

"Not unless they come out of their room."

"Zane found six men with watches like the one I described. I didn't recognize any of them." She picked up her e-reader. "I'll be on the balcony."

Alan changed his clothes. Waiting for two days was stupid. He opened the sliding glass door.

ZoElle looked up. She'd finger combed her hair, and it cascaded in waves around her face. Even without makeup, she was the most beautiful woman he'd ever known.

The words rattling around his head wouldn't come out.

"Did you need something?"

You. The thought shot through him, and he stood paralyzed.

"Alan?" She set the reader in her lap.

"Dinner?" The word came out strangled.

"What?"

"Did you want me to order dinner?"

"No, thank you. I'm not hungry. But don't let that stop you."

Alan sat on the other chair. "Is something wrong?"

"Nothing. Just the stress of being on duty 24/7 for two weeks."

Two weeks of faking newlyweds. "If you would take the bed, you'd get more rest."

"Not revisiting that." ZoElle swiped the screen of her reader. "If it makes you feel better, I'll sleep there Saturday night. Then it won't matter if housekeeping finds furnidents from the pullout couch."

"We could talk about—"

ZoElle held up her hand. "Two more days. I promise—no more small talk. Go get your dinner. I can hear your stomach rumbling from here."

It wasn't. But the elephant in the room couldn't get any bigger.

"Okay." If he were a drinking man, he'd make a toast to another long awkward night.

THE SUITE PHONE RANG TWICE as they were leaving for a late breakfast. Alan answered and handed the receiver to Elle, whispering. "Cassie."

"Hey, Cassie."

"You know the dresses we didn't get to try on yesterday?"

"Can't forget them." Or the obscene price tags.

"Well, Case bought them for me as a surprise. I don't need two. I wondered if you would like one."

Could she expense it? "Sure."

"Why don't you come over and try your dress on. If it fits, we can wear them tonight for the formal."

"We were headed out to breakfast."

"Tell Alan to save a place for you in line. His eyes will pop out when he sees you in it."

Only if he was acting. "Sure. I'll be over in a minute." She hung up the phone.

"Cassie seems to want to talk to me alone again."

Alan frowned. "You sure that's what she wants? She was talking about a dress."

"A $200 sundress that's supposed to make you drool."

"I thought she said 'eyes pop out.'" Alan smiled, and his blue eyes twinkled.

Elle avoided rolling her eyes. "Go save me a place. I'll be down in a few minutes."

"You have your phone?"

"And earrings." Elle double-checked to make sure they were charged in case she needed them later.

"Then I'll see you at breakfast."

At Elle's knock, Case opened the door. So much for Cassie wanting to talk with her alone. "She's in the bedroom."

Cassie sat tied to one of the kitchenette chairs with a sheet. A man in a crew uniform stood behind her holding a long, thin knife at her neck. Tall, lean, and tan—and wearing the watch she couldn't place. He had been working at the information table downstairs. The crew member who shouldn't have been in the elevator the morning Cassie had stormed out. Elle stepped into a better position to free Cassie. If only she could signal Case to let her handle things.

Case grabbed Elle, twisted her arm behind her back, and wrapped his arm around her, pressing a knife to her throat. Case was not being threatened. How had she missed that?

The man behind Cassie spoke. "Two for the price of one. You did well, brother."

So Case had a brother. Elle ran over the options in her mind. She could take out Case, but the man with the knife at Cassie's throat might cut her first. If he hit an artery, there wouldn't be time to save her.

"Don't even think about it." Case twisted her arm higher and forced her into another chair. "This one has some self-defense training. Not just a computer nerd."

They knew her background. Of course. Alan had proven a good web search would show that much. But were they aware of the full extent of her currently useless hand-to-hand combat skills?

"So, ladies, this is how it's going to go down. In case you are too blonde to figure it out, this is a kidnapping. If Cassie's family and

Elle's sister-in-law pay the ransom, the two of you will magically appear dockside at seven thirty Sunday morning. If they don't, your bodies will be found later. Maybe."

Elle adjusted the grip on her phone so she could set off the Hastings app.

"Hey, get her phone." The brother didn't lose his hold on Cassie.

Case ripped the phone from her hand and dumped it and Cassie's into an ice bucket full of water on the dresser. Knowing the phone was waterproof, Elle opened her mouth to yell her safety word, but Case clamped his hand over it, and pressed his knife harder against her neck. "Careful, Mrs. Hastings. My brother said alive, not unhurt. And with your background, I'm sure my brother and I can find some inventive ways to make your worst nightmares come true. We were rather put out by your interference yesterday."

Elle pushed the threat from her mind. She could survive anything if it wasn't her own death.

Cassie's eyes grew wide. "You promised you wouldn't hurt her when you made me call."

"I also promised to love you until death do we part. I lied." Case ran a finger down Elle's cheek. "I've propositioned this beauty several times this week. She has not been as accommodating as the coeds on deck 9."

The color drained from Cassie's face only to be replaced by rage. "You—"

The brother yanked on Cassie's hair, forcing her head back. "Careful, my sweet," he whispered into her ear.

Earrings. Slowly, Elle raised her hand to her right ear, but Case slapped her hand away and yanked out her earring, ripping her earlobe.

Elle swallowed a yelp.

"This should be proof that we have her for her husband. He claimed he gave them to her for her wedding day. She's worn them every day."

"Enough games. Ladies, time for you to disappear." The man behind Cassie moved to the side. Cassie pulled at the sheet binding her to the chair. "I am afraid you must be unconscious for that. We could hit you over the head, but this way is more humane. My doctor brother has concocted a drug that works marvelously. We have tested it many times."

Drugged? Many times? Elle's mind raced, trying to connect the dots.

She should have tried to take the men out. Drugged out of their mind wasn't going to work to get away. She needed to save Cassie regardless of what happened to her, but at this point, she ran more of a risk of getting them both killed.

The brother pointed to two water bottles. "You have two choices. Drink it, or we inject it. We are on a timetable, and we're already five minutes behind."

The brother held a water bottle to Cassie's lips. She turned away, letting the water spill down her front, her act of defiance earning her a slap. "I thought you said she had no spirit. Give her the needle. And you, Mrs. Hastings, drink?"

Elle took the water bottle. The choice was the lesser of the two evils. She would remain with Cassie, and if she didn't finish it, the drug might wear off sooner.

Case opened a drawer and pulled out a syringe. "My dear, if only you had shown such spirit in our bed. This will sting."

Elle brought the bottle to her lips. She let her hand shake, spilling some out.

"Mrs. Hastings. Let me hold it for you." The brother's hand clamped over hers, forcing the bottle between her lips.

Elle didn't need to fake the water dribbling out of her mouth this time.

"Don't worry, you don't need the entire bottle."

Cassie's head bobbed to her chest.

Elle fought to stay in the world fading around her.

"Aw, your ring."

The last thing she felt was her wedding ring sliding off her finger.

In line, Alan allowed another couple to skip ahead of him.

Case came around the corner. "There you are. Cassie says there was a wardrobe malfunction. They'll be here any minute. They said to get a table. Elle wants the waffle and berries."

Alan waved, indicating for a family to pass them in line.

Case glared. "Why did you let them go?"

"It's rude to save places."

"They'll be here in a moment. I'll talk to the maître d', or whatever they call them on the ship." Case butted in front of the family Alan had let pass.

Alan pulled out his phone and checked the Hastings app. ZoElle's phone seemed to be in Cassie's stateroom, although it wasn't transmitting well—a problem they'd had all voyage.

"The next table for four is ours."

"Maybe we should go back and get them and go to the buffet."

"Cassie doesn't like the buffet. Too many people squashed in one space."

The maître d' motioned Case over, then seated them at a window table for four. Alan followed Case's lead and ordered for ZoElle, adding a side of bacon. Odd she hadn't included more protein in her order. She ate some form of protein every morning.

Alan checked the time on his phone. "I'm surprised they're taking so long."

"Girl talk. Cassie can talk the ears off an elephant."

"Elle and I worked out this morning. She hasn't eaten yet." Alan checked his phone screen. Something was off.

"I don't understand how the two of you manage to work out so much on your honeymoon. What kind—" Case stopped talking as a waiter appeared with a silver tray.

"Mr. Johnson? Mr. Hastings?"

"That's us."

"I have these for you. Your breakfast will be delivered to your rooms." The waiter set two pink, one-pound chocolate boxes marked with their names on the table.

"Our wives must be up to something." Case picked up his box and winked.

The box was much lighter than the expected one pound. Something rattled inside.

Case opened his box and gasped.

Alan removed the lid from his and saw the diamond ring Abbie had loaned ZoElle along with one earring, which lay on top of a printed note.

I have your wife. Return to your suite. Alert no one. No phone calls. No texts.

And yes, I have his wife too.

Over their boxes, Alan met Case's frightened eyes.

"What do we do?" asked Case.

"Von Neumann." It was the first time in his life Alan had used this panic word outside a drill. He might not be able to use his phone, but he could send out the alert and start recording and delivering that recording via the Hastings app.

"What?"

"Sorry. Swear word of choice. John von Neumann was a brilliant mathematician who solved the unsolvable." That should be enough to let his parents know something was very wrong. Usually he only talked about von Neumann's work in conjunction with computers.

"How is that going to help with our wives?"

Alan chose his words carefully. "I don't know. They must be on board, and there are cameras everywhere. We'll find them. Let's follow the instructions and return to our rooms."

Instead of a towel animal, an envelope sat in the middle of the made-up bed. Alan took photos of it before opening it and reading it aloud.

Mr. Hastings,

I hope you have enjoyed your new bride enough to want to get her back. How fortunate your sister has access to billions of dollars. She will hardly miss the $10 million it will take to return your wife on Sunday morning dockside. I have enclosed a payment schedule with the amounts and numbers for the transfers. To keep your wife safe:

1. Payments must be completed in the ten-minute window specified. All times are ship time, so make sure your sister does the math.

2. Speak to no one other than Mr. Johnson about this. I know you are a man of action, but your actions will kill her.

3. Only use the room phone to contact your sister.

4. Stay in your room. You are a newlywed. No one expects to see you anywhere else. Your meals will be delivered to your room as will further instructions.

Call your sister now.

Alan rubbed the bridge of his nose. A message popped up on his phone.

Abbie had activated the Hastings app on her cell phone.

Good. His parents were listening. Alan sat down next to the room phone and dialed Abbie. He had to assume his phone was being monitored from this end too.

"Hello?"

"Hey, Abbie. I'm not sure how to tell you this, but ZoElle is being held for $10 million."

Abbie gasped appropriately. Probably a duplicate of the gasp their parents had heard moments ago. "When? What happened?"

"There is another newlywed couple in the cabin next to us. Cassie and Case. This morning, just as we were leaving for breakfast, Cassie called ZoElle to come over about a dress. I went down to the dining room to save us a spot in line. Case joined me, and as we were seated at the table, we received a couple of ransom notes. She'd been gone maybe twenty or thirty minutes."

"Have you contacted anyone?"

"I've been instructed not to."

"How do I get you the money?"

"They left detailed instructions with specific times, amounts, and accounts."

"Not numbers! What if my dysgraphia goofs up the numbers and I send it to the wrong place? You know how I am with numbers." What was she talking about? Abbie never even used a calculator for simple math.

A mechanical voice interrupted the call. "Mrs. Harmon, if you provide an email address, I'll send you a copy. I wouldn't want your sister-in-law to suffer because you got the numbers wrong."

Abbie rattled off an email address that wasn't her normal one. Most likely it was one monitored by Dermott Security.

"How do I know you really have her?" asked Abbie.

"Ask your brother," said the mechanical voice.

"In the box with the kidnapper's note was her diamond ring and one of the earrings I gave her." Alan pulled the earring out of the box. It was the microphone end with the GPS. "She'll feel lost without them."

The voice interrupted. "This call has lasted long enough. Do you have the email, Mrs. Harmon?"

"I don't know. I need to get to a computer."

Silence filled the line.

"Yes, I have the email."

The phone disconnected.

Someone knocked on his door. Alan opened it to find room service with his breakfast. He wasn't hungry anymore.

A flash of panic sent adrenaline coursing through Elle's veins. She blinked twice to be sure her eyes were open. Not even the emergency light showing the location of the room's life jackets glowed. The cloth gag in her mouth was damp with her own saliva. The background hum, the ship's movement, and the soft bed she lay on were the only clues to her location.

Faint, even breaths came from her left, and zip ties encircled her wrists and ankles. Her captors had obliged her by fastening her hands in front of her body. Unfortunately, they had connected them to her feet with a chain of zip ties. The chain allowed some movement, much better than being trussed up like a calf.

The method she usually used to break zip ties was useless. Thankfully, whatever drug it was that they had given her hadn't left her feeling foggy brained. At least she didn't think it had. It was always a risk taking an unknown drug. No point in second-guessing her choices now, though. She could do that when she wrote up the report later.

Elle tested her range of motion. Her feet were not anchored to anything other than her hands. If she straightened her legs, her hands touched her knees. Slowly, she rolled onto her back. Her elbow connected with Cassie. Elle scooted away, trying to locate the edge of the bed, but she didn't want to roll off for fear of coming in contact with the sharp corner of a nightstand.

The bed was wide, so they were most likely not the crew's cabins, which would contain bunk beds for all but the senior staff and officers. That there was no porthole indicated they were in an interior room. Not overly helpful, but it meant they'd been removed from the deck where their suites were since the lounge took up much of the interior space. With how she'd likely been out for more than an hour and the number of cameras on board, it was obvious this operation had been well planned. The question was, would they be released, or would someone take the money and dump them in Davy Jones's locker? Case hadn't hidden his identity.

Not good.

Their lives were only valuable until the ransom was collected. Someone would demand proof that they were alive, but letting them go later would be too risky. Case and his brother intended to kill them. Elle pushed the thought to the back of her mind. Focusing on her death would not help her find a way out.

Elle contemplated removing her gag and screaming for all she was worth, but the chances of anyone being in the surrounding cabins were low. Better if her captors thought she still slept. Someone would be back, even if only to inject them with more of the drug. If she could manage to open the door and get out of the room even a few feet, she was certain a camera would find her. Too risky to Cassie if she couldn't move yet, not to mention their captors might be guarding the door.

Her pen. Elle tried to reach into her pocket and concluded it wasn't possible without her being a contortionist. She twisted another direction as the lone earring bounced against her neck.

The receiver wouldn't do her much good since she couldn't communicate with anyone on the other end. Or could she?

Turning the earrings on caused a pop in the ship's security system. It wasn't Morse code, but it might get someone's attention.

ALAN CHECKED HIS PHONE FOR any updates. Someone needed to spring him from his room. Texts from his mother advising him to appear to follow orders had him grinding his teeth. He circled the stateroom. A soda can sat near the coffeemaker. How had the can gotten there? Neither ZoElle nor he drank soda often. He should put it in the fridge.

As soon as he lifted the can, he knew it wasn't a can at all. He set it in the fridge. The camera would capture a view of water bottles and the breakfast he couldn't eat. If there was one hidden camera, there were bound to be others. Alan paced the room again, hoping that whoever watched wouldn't be suspicious. He found the next camera by the bed. It was a pen that hadn't been there earlier. Alan resisted tossing the spycam in a drawer. Someone would notice if he got rid of them all at once. The one in the bathroom was more subtle. Alan brushed his teeth and washed his hands before dropping the hand towel over the tissue box concealing a camera facing the shower.

He wanted to punch the wall.

Wait.

Why was he going along with their demands? ZoElle may be in danger, but she wasn't helpless. Far from it. Either she'd chosen to be kidnapped with Cassie or the situation was much too dire for him to be worried about hidden cameras.

His parents were already working on the outside and had contacted Peter, Zane, the chief security officer, and the FBI. Some law from around the year 2000 gave them oversight to crimes against U.S. citizens on cruise ships if the country the ship sailed under allowed it. Basically, he had a team already working outside his cabin. Alan needed to be with them.

He opened his computer bag and took out the handheld detector he used to sweep the suite once a day. He found a camera disguised as a USB charger and a camera attached to the top of a picture frame. Alan added them and the pen to the one in the refrigerator. The tissue-box cover was too large for the fridge, so he stuffed it into the microwave before leaving his suite and pounding on Case's door.

"What ya' doin'?" Case waved the glass of amber liquid he held in his hand. "We're supposed to stay in our rooms."

"I came to look for clues. My ransom note said I could talk to you. This was the last place Elle was. There has got to be a clue."

"Doubt it. Housekeeping's been here. They even hung up the dresses the girls were trying on." Case waved Alan into the suite.

A room sweep revealed no hidden cameras. So the kidnappers were more afraid of Alan than Case. Made sense. Other than the bottle of liquor on the table, the room was pristinely clean. ZoElle's phone had long since stopped transmitting, but this was the last place it had been.

"Told you there was nothing here. Her goons already came in to look. Got here before I even finished talking to her father. Where were they when my wife disappeared?"

A dozen responses buzzed through Alan's head. He analyzed each one with the speed of the latest Ogilvie computer processor. Feigning ignorance won out. "I thought they were supposed to leave her alone on ship."

"They are. But we still run into them enough."

"It's a small ship."

Case grunted and drained his glass. "The note said not to go to anyone. I don't want to get her killed."

"Her bodyguards know. Captain Wagner knows by now, and someone will have contacted the FBI."

"The FBI? Are you sure?" Case paled and his slurred speech momentarily became clear.

How drunk was he? Where did he get the alcohol? ZoElle said Cassie had had the minibar cleared out. "Yes, the FBI has jurisdiction over shipboard crime against Americans."

"I didn't know that. Do you think they'll come help?"

"Depends. The ship is sailing under Bahama's flag, and we are still someplace south of Cuba. There will be negotiations first. Your wife is too high profile, and the cruise line and the Bahamas won't want the publicity. After a couple rounds of politics, they'll invite agents on board, probably by tomorrow morning."

"What about your wife? Would the FBI come for her?"

"ZoElle isn't high profile enough on her own to make for an easy negotiation, but my brother-in-law is ..." How had he not made the connection? He'd put her in danger. Adam, Alex, and Andrew's wives already had security. Alan's wife and children would make easier targets than his siblings. His mind froze on the mental picture that thought brought up. Two blonde, curly-haired daughters with his wife's stormy gray-blue eyes, a son perched on ZoElle's hip. The rightness of the scene overwhelmed him. He should have told her last night how he felt. Because he wanted her as his future. "I'm going to talk to security. Want to come?"

Case poured himself another drink. "I'm follow'n orders. Y'all can risk your wife's life if ya want."

I'll never skip another yoga class again. Elle's muscles ached from the tiny ball she'd contorted her body into so she could reach her earring. She pinched the earring to turn on the comms. She counted to ten, then turned it off. Counted to ten, then turned it on. She listened for any voice, then tried again. She prayed someone in security would notice the little pops.

After several tries, her back was screaming, so she left the comms in what she hoped was on mode and lowered her feet back to the bed.

Next to her, Cassie continued to sleep.

"Elle?" Jethro's voice came over the comms. "If you hear me, turn the power off and on again."

She curled back up into a ball so fast she hit her nose on her knee. Her fingers fumbled with the earring.

"There you are. We know you don't have the mic, so we are going to have to play twenty questions. For *yes*, turn the power off and on. For *no*, don't do anything. Do you understand?"

Off. On.

"Do you know where you are?"

Elle waited for the next question.

"Are you with Cassie?"

Off. On.

"Are you injured?"

Elle waited.

"Is Cassie?"

How should she answer? She turned the comms off, then counted to ten before turning it back on.

"If that was a *maybe*, repeat the sequence."

"I don't know" was close enough to *maybe* to repeat the slow off, on.

"I will assume since you haven't already escaped that you don't think you can and bring Cassie with you. I'm going to turn the mic over to the head of ship security. We want to see if we can narrow down the search."

A slightly accented voice came over the comms. "Is there any light where you are?"

Not even a bit.

"Is the room carpeted?"

Elle gave the "I don't know" signal.

"Is there a bed in the room?

Off. On.

Elle strained to hear the next question. None came.

She tried turning the comms off and on again.

Nothing.

The power couldn't be drained already, could it?

When she got back to Chicago, she would have a serious conversation with Colin on how to improve his invention.

Someone swore as Alan entered the security room. The chief security officer removed a set of headphones.

"Her signal is gone."

Jethro waved Alan over to where he sat. "We had Elle on her comms."

"I thought she only had the receiver."

"She got our attention by turning it off and on. She must have drained the power."

Another defect to report to Colin.

"What did you learn?" Alan sank into a seat.

"Cassie may be injured. They are together. It's dark. And they are most likely in a stateroom, not a crew room." The security officer rubbed the back of his neck. "All we needed was ten minutes more. We planned to run an emergency-light test to figure out what section of the ship she was in.

"How would that have worked?" asked Alan.

"All the suites have a low-level emergency light near the door. We were going to run the tests in sections to see when she saw the light."

Jethro leaned forward in his seat. "We should get you caught up on the timeline."

Someone cued up the security tape from the morning. The film started with the arrival of one of the stewards ten minutes before Elle knocked on the door. "Why did they call the steward to their room?"

The chief security officer stopped the video. "Actually, he's a junior purser. There was a computer error on Mr. and Mrs. Johnson's bill. Mr. Johnson took exception to the $10,000 charge. We've interviewed the purser. He said the women went into the bedroom and closed the door. He didn't see them again, and he left with Mr. Johnson, which corroborates with what Mr. Johnson told Peter." He restarted the video. "Housekeeping comes through six minutes after Mr. Johnson leaves the room. We've interviewed both employees. Both claim the room was empty. Although they would have had no reason to look in the closets."

Alan rubbed his temples. "Then how did they disappear?"

A PAIN-FILLED MOAN EMANATED FROM Cassie.

Elle worked her way to the edge of the bed. She needed room to stand if she wanted to break the zip ties. The bed was big enough that Elle decided there was no bunk bed above it. She placed her feet on the floor, wrists between her knees. With her teeth, she tightened the zip tie around her wrists as much as possible. Getting any of the zip ties to break would be a win. Attempting something akin to a cannonball to jumping jack seemed like the best plan.

It would either work, or she'd fall on her face.

Three. Elle brought her knees up until she was in a tight ball.

Two. Deep breath.

One. She exploded. If the gag hadn't been in her mouth, her muffled scream would have been heard all over the deck.

Snap. Her arms flew up, hands still linked, free from her legs, but her relief was short-lived as her ankles stayed together, her left foot feeling like it had landed on a porcupine or cup of tacks. Her shoulder slammed into a wall, her head following. Pain shot from her shoulder to the center of her body, and she crumpled to the floor.

So not part of the plan. Elle brought her hands to her face and tried to remove the gag. It was on too tight. She needed her hands free. Hands no longer connected to her feet, she could break the zip ties in the way she'd practiced a thousand times.

Using the wall, Elle stood and lifted her wrists over her head. Bringing her arms down fast, she broke the zip tie. Pain shot through her left shoulder again. Elle rubbed it with her right hand. Her shoulder was swelling. Biting against the pain, she reached behind her head to untie the gag. Then she worked her jaw. Now for her feet. If only she had her trusty pen. It had either fallen out of her pocket or been removed. The long hook on her earring should do the trick.

She felt for the little cube-shaped lock at the end of the zip tie and worked the earring post to release the tab, a move she'd practiced a hundred times with similar tools. Once her feet were free, she stood unsteadily, half expecting to find more of whatever she'd landed on earlier, but the carpet was soft beneath her feet.

Cassie moaned again, only the pitch changed and she started thrashing about.

"Cassie? We will be okay. I've broken free. I need to find a light. Stay still so you don't hurt yourself." Elle put as much confidence into her voice as she could and tried to hold her own tears back. Her shoulder throbbed. Ignoring the pain was all she could do for now.

The moaning quieted.

"Concentrate on taking deep breaths through your nose." As Elle felt along the wall, searching with both hands for furniture and other objects, her fingers found a hinge and a smooth door. A bathroom? There must be a light switch. Finding none on either side of the door, Elle opened it and was greeted by the smell of cleanser and musty water. Four inches into the room, her fingers found a light switch. She turned away as the low-wattage bulb momentarily blinded her.

She surveyed the small room. Cassie lay on the bed, wide eyes begging for help, tears running down her face. Elle stepped away from the bathroom door only to have it close automatically behind her. She propped it open with a wastebasket.

Elle stepped over Cassie's sandals. Obviously not a porcupine. The designer who thought the metal studs were a good idea, never stepped on his creation in the dark. "Let's get out of here. I'll take your gag off, but you need to stay as quiet as possible. We don't know who or what is on the other side of the door."

"This isn't a nightmare, is it? My husband—" Cassie bit her lip, trying to contain her sobs.

"We'll get out of here." Elle used her earring to remove the zip ties binding Cassie. "Sit up slowly. You got more of the drug than I did. Are you dizzy?"

Cassie shook her head. "How did you get free?"

"Lots of training. I'm one of your bodyguards."

"You mean you're spending your honeymoon guarding me?"

"We aren't married." Elle worked the zip ties on Cassie's ankles.

"If you're a bodyguard, why didn't you take them out in the suite?"

"The knife at your throat was too big a risk. I decided staying with you was the best path." She'd planned on having both her earrings and being rescued before waking up. "How do you feel?"

"Physically? A little bruised. Emotionally? I'll save the emotional breakdown for later."

"Put on your shoes and stay close to me. If I say run, scream your head off and run like your junior high PE teacher is after you. The security crew is watching the cameras. If you can find an elevator, all the better." Elle put on her own shoes.

"I shouldn't leave you."

Elle checked the hallway through the fish-eye peephole. Empty. "If I tell you to run, it's because I'm fighting our captors. You'll help me more by attracting the attention of the crew and your other bodyguards to wherever we are."

"Okay." The squeak from Cassie was hardly convincing.

"Ready?" Elle put her hand on the doorknob and turned it.

The door wouldn't open.

Six hours. Alan studied the map of the next deck they would clear. It was a slow process and one they had hoped to avoid. If they didn't find them, the captain had authorized a muster drill as a last resort. Although since the crew members were involved with the kidnapping, there was a chance the muster drill still wouldn't locate the women as one of the kidnappers could be the one assigned to check the stateroom or crew cabin where the women were being held.

"There are seven vacant staterooms on this deck," said the security member accompanying Alan as they reached the bottom of the next stairway.

Two of the Sassy Seniors stood in front of the elevators. "Hey, lover boy, where is your wife?"

"Hush, Linda, can't you see he's with ship security?" said Annie.

"Don't shush me just because I don't know all the uniforms like you do."

"I still say it was a purser helping housekeeping."

"What?" the crew member and Alan voiced in unison.

"Annie claims she saw the cute purser who helped us change our last excursion doing housekeeping. She has hot men on her mind."

"He was wearing the wrong uniform." Annie crossed her arms.

"When was this?" asked Alan.

"This morning. I slept in and had to go for a late breakfast. I tried to say hello, but he ignored me."

"Where?" The security member pulled out a paper map.

"The same deck as the good breakfast restaurant. Wait. No, I was on the wrong floor. I keep getting this ship confused with our last one."

"Annie doesn't know port from aft. But if she walks in circles long enough, she will eventually get to where she wants to be."

Annie shot Linda a glare. "I was one deck too high, so I was on nine. They were coming out of the employee area with two carts."

"What time was this?"

"I'm not sure. I missed the crepe bar, and it closes at ten. Why do you ask?"

Alan exchanged a look with the security guard. "I've lost something, and you may have given us a clue."

"Oh, goodie. I love clues." Linda beamed. "As long as you didn't lose your wife. That would be tragic."

Alan clenched his jaw to keep from saying that *tragic* wasn't a strong enough word.

"Thank you, ladies." The security guard started down the steps to the deck below.

Alan updated Jethro through his comms.

"What do we do now?" Cassie's voice quivered.

"Plan B. We wait for them to come to us." Elle scanned the room for anything she could use as a weapon.

"What if they don't come?"

"They will. They know the drugs will wear off. They can't risk us pounding on the walls or anything. They'll be back to give us more"

"I still can't believe my husband—I mean Case—would do this to me. I thought he was different and that—" Cassie covered her face.

Elle hugged her with her good arm. "You thought you could trust your heart?"

Cassie nodded.

You and me both.

When something scraped against the door, Elle raised her finger to her mouth in the universal sign for silence. "Stay flat against the wall and be ready to run."

The door opened. Elle recognized Case's brother before his hand touched the light switch. Her first kick caught him in the gut, doubling him over. With her good arm, she spun him into the wall. "Run!"

Cassie dashed out of the room. "Help! Help!"

Their captor swung at Elle, hitting her injured shoulder. Despite the white-hot pain flashing through her, she grabbed the doorjamb, propelling herself into the hallway. Another blow landed on her back, slamming her face-first into the wall opposite the door.

She screamed as he grabbed her left arm and wrenched it behind her, further straining her shoulder. She hadn't been in this much pain since the night her former boss had tried to kill her. Elle struggled to think of her next move. Over a year of training for hand-to-hand combat and this was where she'd ended up? What was the point if she couldn't break free? She kicked her leg back, missing his shin.

He forced her arm up higher and pressed a knife against the back of her neck. "Stop or I'll kill you now."

The wave of pain that burst through her threatened to drown her, and she fought to remain upright and conscious.

Then she felt the knife at her throat.

"Help! Help!"

With the security guard close behind him, Alan ran down the narrow hallway toward the screaming.

Cassie rounded a corner, barreling into Alan.

"Help her." Alan passed Cassie to the security officer.

"Turn left," said the voice in his headset. They must have ZoElle on camera.

Alan skidded to a stop. There in front of him, the junior purser held a knife to her throat.

He dragged ZoElle back a step. She winced, her breath coming in barely controlled puffs.

"Back up, and she won't get hurt."

Alan took a step back. A cornered man was a dangerous man.

"I want my money. And a helicopter out of here."

"It isn't time for the wire transfer yet." Alan kept his voice calm to give the security team time to move into position.

"I don't care. You and your intrusive wife ruined our plans three times on this trip."

ZoElle's head wobbled. Was it a ruse or was she going to faint? Either way, she'd distracted her captor. Alan took a step closer. ZoElle yelped. There was no mistaking the pain or the sheen of sweat on her face.

"I told you to keep back." The junior purser pressed the blade into ZoElle's throat, and a line of red appeared below the point. A commotion at the end of the hall caused the captor to look behind him.

"I told you not to drink that last cocktail. Let's get you to bed." Melanie pulled a wobbly Jethro behind her, scolding and clucking at him. She didn't look up until she was five feet away from ZoElle. "Oh, my! What are you doing to that poor girl?"

As the captor loosened his grip on the knife, Alan lunged for the man's knife arm at the same time Jethro took a swipe at the man's legs. ZoElle screamed and collapsed, and Jethro slammed the man against the wall. Melanie pulled a pair of handcuffs from her oversized beach bag.

The hall flooded with security personnel.

Alan frantically searched for something to stanch the blood oozing from ZoElle's neck.

"Ship's doctor. Let me through."

When the words didn't register, someone grabbed Alan's shoulder and pulled him back.

"Let the doctor in, son." His father's voice pierced the fog of fear. Alan stood and joined his parents. The purser was already gone.

She couldn't die. He needed to tell her. He watched helplessly as ZoElle was transferred to a gurney and whisked away.

"Go with her." His mom gave him a shove.

Alan obeyed.

WAITING-ROOM CHAIRS WERE UNCOMFORTABLE EVEN on a cruise ship. There must be some universal law demanding the injustice. Text after text came in over the Hastings app as the story unfolded and the rest of the participants were rounded up. Alan wished he'd punched Case the first time he'd flirted with ZoElle. He wouldn't have the chance to punch him now. A US Coast Guard helicopter out of Puerto Rico would land any minute to take Case, his brother, and their accomplices into custody. The FBI had easily won the jurisdictional spitting match after everyone realized the kidnappers were also US citizens.

Alan didn't care about any of it. He stared at the door leading back into the medical rooms, waiting for any news.

More texts from his siblings came through, all of them wishing Elle well. Adam was back in the office with Alex. Andrew and Jordan texted from their honeymoon. Abbie sent her love and told Alan to get ZoElle something special from the shops, her treat. Alan didn't answer them. He couldn't.

The door to the back room opened, and the doctor came out. "Mr. Hastings? Come with me."

To his surprise, Alan was ushered into an empty exam room. "Your wife will be fine. The cut wasn't deep, and she didn't lose much blood, but she has a severely dislocated shoulder. I've done what I can, but she may need surgery. I advise she get an MRI as soon as possible. My biggest worry is her amnesia."

"Amnesia?"

"Yes. She insists she isn't married."

Alan stared at his wedding band. "She isn't."

"According to the ship manifest, you are married. You realize that's fraud?"

"The captain and head of security are aware of the situation. We were undercover bodyguards for Cassie Johnson, or Evans."

"If you aren't married, this conversation is over. Patient privacy. I hope you understand."

"May I see her?"

"She requested not. Had she been your spouse…" The doctor shrugged.

"I understand."

"I have a new problem now. I need to send her back to her stateroom. We try not to keep patients overnight, but I don't want her being alone."

"My mother is on the cruise. I could switch rooms with her if ZoElle agrees."

"I'll be back."

Alan sent his mother a private message. **We will need your help in the room when they release her.**

—I was already planning on it. Elle may need more care than you should give.

I'll let you know when we are leaving here.

—Okay.

The doctor returned. "Miss Watson agrees to your arrangement. I'll arrange for transport."

"I'll walk her up."

"I'll ask Miss Watson." The doctor left again.

Alan prayed that whatever pain meds ZoElle was on would make her less stubborn.

Elle took a deep breath. Alan was the last person she wanted to see, but she'd already caused enough trouble for everyone. Surgery. She wouldn't be able to start with Dermot for at least two months. If they would still have her after the colossal failure of the day. She'd come close to getting them killed.

The nurse assisted her off the table. "Here's a written copy of your instructions. I suggest you get your hair washed at the spa and avoid showers to keep your neck dry."

"Good idea. What should I do with this shirt?" Elle tugged at the oversized pink shirt they'd loaned her.

"Keep it. We keep a few cruise T-shirts around here for situations like this. Kind of a perk for being ill." The nurse held out a blue plastic bag. "You're sure you want to keep this?"

"They may need my shirt for evidence."

"I'll take it." Alan stood in the doorway. His hair stood on end. He'd been running his hands through it. He held open the doors while protecting her left side. But he didn't touch her. They managed to find an empty elevator.

"Someone will want to interview me, right?"

"I suppose so."

"Will you please help me get this conversation with Jethro and Melanie over with as soon as possible? I want to tell my story once and then take the pain pills. I only let them give me a local in my shoulder."

"May I be there?"

"You're my partner. This is work. You deserve to know." Every stupid detail of my failure so you can finally say "I told you so."

The elevator stopped at their deck. Alan let her exit first but still didn't touch her. She tried to tell herself it was for the best. If he put his arm around her, she'd crumble and lose her last shred of dignity.

He opened the door to the suite. "Mom should be here in a moment. Cassie is finishing her interviews."

"How is she?" Focusing on the client would help her keep moving.

"I don't know. Do you need anything?"

"Did someone make sure Cassie's eaten something? I don't think she had breakfast either."

"Do you want food?" His blue eyes searched hers as they had when they'd first met. He must be afraid she'd start crying. Not this time. Not in front of him.

Elle turned so that she didn't have to keep looking at the eyes that would haunt her for the rest of her life. If September wrote a song about the Hastings's blue eyes, Elle would boycott her after she downloaded the single to every device she had.

Alan moved close behind her. "ZoElle—"

"Stop!" She whirled to face him. "I've asked you a million times. Call me Elle. Why can't you do that one simple thing for me? Call me Elle like the rest of my friends."

"I can't."

"Why not?" Yes! A reason to be angry with him. Anger was easier.

"*Elle* means 'her.'"

"Congratulations. You know your French pronouns."

"You aren't just another her. You aren't a pronoun. I can't think of you as another her. Anyone can be her, but you are the only you."

"But—" She had no argument for that. The thought was so, so romantic, which was proof the pain was playing with her mind. Alan wasn't romantic.

Someone knocked on their door. Alan answered it. Elle sunk into the upholstered chair as Jethro, Melanie, Cassie, her bodyguards, the head of security, the captain, and two other men in business suits she didn't recognize came in.

Melanie and Cassie were the first to reach Elle. Cassie crouched down in front of her. "Thank you. I'd hug you, but I don't want to hurt you."

Elle reached out and gave her a half hug.

Melanie sat down on the end of the coffee table. "Cassie can't stay to listen to your statement. I've agreed to stay with her for the next hour. Will you be good with Jethro and Alan for now?"

Elle nodded. "I need to wash my hair. There's still blood in it."

"According to Alan's text, the nurse told you to wash your hair at the spa so your neck wouldn't get wet. I'll make an appointment."

More people to see her. Elle bit her lip. The smell of her own blood was nauseating. "I guess that is best. I won't be able to sleep until it's washed though."

"Jethro will text us when you're done."

Before or after she was fired?

As ZoElle's tale unfolded, Alan wished he'd mastered Adam's impassive bodyguard face. Willingly drinking a drug was incredibly stupid. And undeniably brave. And under the circumstances, the wisest choice.

"So, when you woke up, you didn't feel groggy?" asked one of the suits.

"No more than on a Monday at 5:00 a.m."

The other man typed on his phone. "And you say Dr. Case Johnson formulated it?"

"That's what his brother said. The one dressed as a crew member. I don't know his name, but I saw him at the information booth, and he followed Cassie on the elevator once."

"Go on with your story."

When she reached the part about breaking the zip ties, they stopped her again. "So your shoulder injury was not caused by your assailants?"

"The initial injury was my fault. I miscalculated. The pain wasn't terrible. I could work through that, but when he twisted my arm back, the pain multiplied."

"Go on."

ZoElle concluded her story and answered their questions.

"Do you know how they got you out of the room?" asked the head of security.

ZoElle closed her eyes, the space between her brows crinkling. "There were two laundry bags on the bed. Considering my unexplained bruises. I assume they folded us up with the sheets. Which reminds me—did you find my phone?"

"We are fairly sure both phones went overboard."

"Oh." Elle shifted in her seat, her breathing deliberately slow. How much longer could she last before she could take the pain medication?

"It was one of our first tips that Case Johnson was involved," said the head of security. "After he came back from breakfast, he went out on the deck and was talking on the phone. Then he tripped, and the phone went overboard. We have a few of those each cruise. Only ten minutes later, when Peter and Zane went to the room to check on Cassie's whereabouts, he had his phone in his back pocket. Unfortunately, we didn't connect the two incidents for a while."

"They had a decent plan. There's a blind spot in the cameras for two feet on either side of the doorway to the room you were in. The room was listed as booked on the ship's computer, but housekeeping listed it as empty on their roster because it was indeed empty when we left LA. The room was stocked with zip ties, water, packaged foods, and vials of an unknown drug. At least one of the accomplices was staying in the room prior to the kidnapping and posing as housekeeping."

The captain stood along with the other men. "Miss Watson, we owe you our thanks for saving Ms. Evans. Without your bold actions, it would have taken several more hours to find you. We planned a muster drill to empty all the rooms, but the real housekeeping assigned to that area wouldn't have checked an unoccupied room. If there's anything you need for the rest of the trip, please let us know."

The crew and men in suits left, and Jethro held up his phone. "Melanie says she needs more time with Cassie. She's made the appointment for you to get your hair washed at the spa. Would you like me to walk you down?"

"I can go myself."

"As your boss, I am going to overrule you. With the Coast Guard helicopter landing, rumors are running rampant. For your privacy and safety, you are getting an escort."

ZoElle's shoulder slumped. "I understand." She weaved a bit as she stood. Alan reached to steady her, but she sidestepped him. "I was going to wait until Monday, but I'm turning in my two weeks' notice. The email with it was in my phone. I'll send it as soon as I can get to my cloud."

When Alan opened his mouth to tell ZoElle not to be stupid, Jethro shook his head ever so slightly, stopping him.

"I accept your resignation on one condition. Hastings Security will pay for all of your resulting medical bills and rehabilitation as well as medical leave until you are able to work elsewhere, even if your recovery takes more than two months."

"Thank you. That's very generous." Her voice wobbly, ZoElle adjusted her sling.

Alan doubted ZoElle realized his father was effectively keeping her hired for the next two months. He stood mutely as he watched Jethro and ZoElle leave.

NEVER HAD A HAIR WASHING felt so good as the warm water flowed over Elle's scalp. The cosmetologist wouldn't let Elle apologize for the blood. Elle relaxed into the massage and the exotic shampoo's soothing vanilla-and-jasmine scent. Soon she was sitting up in front of the stylist's mirror.

"How would you like your hair done?"

Something to signal a change in her life. "I was thinking about cutting it chin length. Do you have time?"

"Time, yes, but I won't cut off more than a half inch."

"Why not?"

"Trauma cuts turn into big regrets. I am not cutting off eight inches of hair when you've had an awful day."

So much for washing that man right out of her hair. She needed a big, drastic change.

"However, I am the best braider on the ship. Let me put in some braids I guarantee will last three days. Then you won't have to deal with your hair until you are back on land."

The beautician was right. Cutting her hair wasn't going to erase Alan from her memory. "Please, the braids sound workable."

Elle let her mind wander. Deidre would hear about her injury from Adam or Alex and tell Liam. If Dermot Security was willing to let her work a desk job, she would be able to start on time unless she required surgery. Oh no—her parents. What would they say? They'd been against her becoming a bodyguard from day one. There was always Colin's offer to join C&O as a programmer.

Even if she could get an MRI in Florida, she would still need a doctor in Chicago. If she cut her visit short or canceled it entirely, she'd never hear the end of it. Going back to Chicago would mean Alan, and she didn't need to go back to being the poor woman who needed rescuing. She didn't need the pitying looks. Jethro had a better bodyguard face, which didn't make her look forward to her exit interview. She didn't need him to tell her how she'd messed up. She should have seen the red flags signaling Case's involvement—his irritation when she'd returned to the ship early with Cassie after the dress incident, the too-alert drunk.

"There. What do you think?"

"Cute. Thanks. It will help to not have to worry about my hair."

Jethro waited near the check-in desk. He cleared the way to the elevator, which was full. So they waited for another. It was full too.

"We can take the stairs," said Elle.

"Are you up to it?"

"It's only two flights." The stairs were usually empty.

The room was empty. Alan's laptop wasn't on the table.

Jethro sat down on the couch. "I know we said Melanie would be here, but Cassie is having difficulty with the situation."

"I understand. She's our client. Don't worry. I don't need a bodyguard in the room. I promise not to open the door to anyone I don't know."

"According to the papers you brought back from the medical center, that isn't an option."

"Once I take the pain meds, I'll be out for the night. I'll be fine." Alone time will be a good thing. Having her former boss in the room was awkward. Boss or not, he was Alan's dad, and somehow that was different from Alan's mom.

"What do you want for dinner?"

"Chicken anything and vegetables. And chocolate anything."

Elle slipped into the bathroom while Jethro picked up the room phone and ordered. Alan's shaving kit was gone. His side of the closet was empty.

Elle pinched her eyes closed. The real reason she needed Jethro gone was so she could cry.

The fastest way to get dinner was through the buffet. Alan stood in line for the meat of the night.

"Where's your wife?"

"I heard they injured her."

"Is she what you were looking for?"

"I told you the purser was in the wrong uniform."

Alan pasted on a smile and turned toward the Sassy Seniors, who were dressed in coordinating but not matching sequined dresses. "It's a long story."

"Then sit with us and share."

There wasn't a polite way out of this. They would hunt him down. Worse, they would hunt ZoElle down. "Sure, I'll sit with you."

They found one of the round bench tables.

"I need to sit on the end, can't scoot in. Bad hip."

"Left-handed. I get the other end."

Alan ended up trapped in the middle. The worst place for a bodyguard. If these four ladies ever chose to live a life of crime, they had the moves down.

"Okay, spill."

"ZoElle and I were undercover. She isn't my wife. The woman we were guarding had some trouble. ZoElle saved her."

Linda's smile disappeared. "I thought you said it was a long story."

"He's a man. That is a long story." Annie winked at him.

"So why are you here instead of with Elle?" asked Georgia.

Alan focused on his food. "She doesn't want me around."

"When did she say this?" asked Pat.

"When we were in the medical center."

Linda pointed her fork at Alan's chest. "She said, 'Hot, fake husband, go walk the plank?'"

"Did you know walking the plank is an author thing? Didn't really happen. I watched a history show."

"Not now, Georgia. We need to know about Elle, not about pirate history."

Alan used his knife to push the tines of Linda's fork away from his heart. "ZoElle wouldn't tell me to jump ship. She told the doctor she didn't want visitors, and I wasn't her husband."

"You sure look like her husband."

"Those smoldering looks."

"Whenever my husband looked at me like that, I knew there would be another baby."

"She'd know. She has eight children."

"And the way she looked at him."

Linda held up her phone. "Does that kiss look fake?"

"Nope."

"Definitely not."

"I felt the sparks rolling off them."

"Better than a rom-com movie."

"Much more convincing than their newlywed friends."

"Never liked him. She was so sweet, and he had roving eyes."

"They tried to hide him when they took him off in the chopper. Did you see that?" asked Georgia.

Alan swallowed his food. "I was in medical with ZoElle."

"Why don't you call her Elle like everyone else?" asked Pat.

Linda rolled her eyes. "Obviously because *Elle* means "her." And she isn't another woman. She's special."

Alan nearly choked on whatever food he'd stuffed in his mouth.

Anne turned to Linda and stage whispered. "Look at him. He's miserable."

"That's because he never told her." Linda's stage whisper back was almost as loud as her normal voice.

"Told her what?" asked Alan.

The Sassy Seniors answered in unison. "That you're in love with her."

They weren't wrong.

Around nine, assisted by the too-short couch, Elle convinced Jethro to leave. He gave her a spare phone and made her promise to use her panic word if she needed anything, including a glass of water.

Elle wasn't stupid. She knew he would probably take up residence in a chair in the private lobby, ten feet beyond the door. He'd be in the room before the last syllable of "Tim Berners-Lee" made it out of her mouth. She'd choose a new word at Dermot. She'd only chosen Mr. Berners-Lee's name because she felt he hadn't gotten the credit he deserved, and the panic word matched Alan's word in an odd sort of way. Granted, the designer of the World Wide Web might not have anything on the creators of the computer, but he had an incredible mind.

She'd kept the shirt Alan had loaned her when Case dumped the drink down her front at the bottom of the dresser drawer. She would return it tomorrow, but tonight, she desperately needed one of his hugs and to sit on the chaise lounge, cradled in his arms. Alan would hold her in a way her shoulder could rest and without the inevitable nightmares.

In the bathroom, she took two of the pain pills she'd been denying herself all day. The shot the doctor had given her in her shoulder had worn off hours ago. She'd taken this prescription before and knew it would knock her out. What little pride she had left had kept her from falling apart in front of her boss. Thankfully, he hadn't taken the opportunity to tell her what she'd done wrong.

Not activating her earrings sooner.

Not shouting "Tim Berners-Lee" to activate her phone.

Not realizing something was off when Case opened the door.

The stupid move that had dislocated her shoulder.

Letting Case's brother use her as a hostage.

Drugging herself.

When she told Liam the truth, Dermot wouldn't want her either.

Case and his brother could have hurt or killed them both. They could have followed through on their not-so-veiled threats. At least she'd kept those out of her testimony. Alan would have gone ballistic. He didn't understand that saving Cassie's life had been worth the calculated risk.

Elle took the sling off and held her arm as still as she could while she changed out of the pink "I love to cruise" T-shirt the nurse had given her. A shower would be nice, but Elle dismissed the idea. If she fell in the shower, Jethro would be the one to rescue her.

Alan's T-shirt reached midthigh and felt like a warm hug. It was baggy enough to hide her lack of a bra, even without the sling back in place. It was harder to swap out her capris for a pair of pajama pants. By the time she finished brushing her teeth, the pills kicked in forcing a yawn.

Elle lined up several pillows on her left side to prevent her from rolling over into her favorite sleeping position during the night and let the pain pills drag her down into sleep.

THE LOBBY WAS QUIET OTHER than his father's snoring. Alan sat across from Jethro and counted. He reached five before his dad woke, fully alert.

"Five seconds."

"I'm an old man. I'm not used to this anymore." Jethro checked his phone." What are you doing here at 2:00 a.m.? Your shift doesn't start until eight."

"I couldn't sleep."

"You're not still on the should-haves, are you? We talked about this earlier. Neither of you thought you would run into danger in Cassie's room."

"It's not that." He rubbed his hand down his face and laughed. "The Sassy Seniors managed to trap me in the center of one of the round booths at dinner. Those ladies are dangerous. There isn't a single move I've learned that I could use to evade them."

"It's the grandma vibe. Your mom has been working on it for years. Our grandkids don't stand a chance of getting away with anything, even though she spoils them to death."

"I still can't believe they maneuvered me to where I couldn't get out." It had been a long, uncomfortable hour and a half where they'd done everything but beat him over the head with Georgia's cane as they gave him advice on how to win ZoElle's heart. It all came down to saying three little words, which scared him almost as bad as when he'd realized she'd been kidnapped.

"Did they give you any good advice?"

"They told me I should tell ZoElle how I feel about her."

Jethro raised a brow. "And?"

"I love her." The words didn't hurt as much as he thought they would.

"How long?"

"I'm not sure. When she flipped me on my back down at the Art House last spring as I was fighting with Alex over his marriage to Kimberly? Or maybe the first time I saw her hold Harmony last February, and I had a stupid thought about what a good mother she'd be?"

"It's been a long time in coming."

"I know, but now she hates me. We had a fight the other night. I wasn't surprised when she gave notice. I'm sure she'd already talked to Liam about a job."

"There is a fine line between love and hate. Elle's been protecting herself for a long time. I don't know as much about women as your mother does, but I think Elle chose to cross that line to protect herself. Hating you was easier than rejection."

"I have not rejected her."

Jethro crossed his arms, waiting.

Alan wanted to squirm like a little kid. "Not really. I've been maintaining a professional distance."

"You have the highest IQ of all my kids and the least common sense."

"I wasn't looking for love. I need more time."

"Once this ship docks, you'll be out of time. You've got one day."

"But she's on pain meds."

"Maybe to sleep. She avoided taking them all evening. The only way I could get her to take them was if I promised to leave the room."

"How do you know she's okay?"

"I set the Hastings app to listen."

"And she left the phone on?"

"I think she put it in a drawer. I may have left a bug behind the bedside lamp."

"You can't listen in on her."

"The contracts say we have the right to monitor all our on-duty employees for their safety."

"She's sleeping."

"And she's on duty until Cassie is safely off this ship." Jethro's soft smile was fatherly.

"You haven't been monitoring our room before now, have you?" There wasn't anything to hide other than the arguments.

"Haven't felt the need. Should I have been making sure you two didn't murder each other?" The corner of Jethro's mouth lifted into a half grin.

"No. All you would have heard was deafening silence."

A painful moan came from Jethro's phone. Jethro stood. "Three a.m. It's been six hours since she had her pain pills. Better go give her some more before she wakes up completely."

"I'll go do it."

"You sure?"

"Don't worry. I'll be a perfect gentleman."

"Never been worried about your behavior." Jethro tapped his phone. "FYI—the bug is now inactive."

Moonlight coming through the balcony windows illuminated the rooms. Alan grabbed a water bottle from the fridge. He found the prescription bottle on the bathroom counter and checked the dosage before removing two pills.

A sharp gasp came from the other room. Alan left the bathroom light on so he could see better.

"Oh, ratzelfratzle."

He tried not to laugh at ZoElle's choice of swear words as he sat down on the edge of the bed. "Here, sweetheart, take these and you can go back to sleep."

"What are you doing here?" With her good arm, she pushed herself up from her nest of pillows."

"Bringing you your 3:00 a.m. painkillers."

"But—"

"Take the pain killers, Elle."

"What?"

"I said take your meds."

"No. You called me Elle." She took the pills from his palm and popped them into her mouth, followed by a long drink.

Alan took the water bottle back. "I decided that if you hated the name ZoElle, I shouldn't use it."

Wincing, she lay back on the pillows.

"Can I help you?" Alan walked around the bed and adjusted the pillows. "Better?"

"Not really, but the meds will put me to sleep in a few minutes, and it won't matter."

"It will matter if you aren't comfortable."

"Why?" She sat up.

"Because you matter, Elle."

A pillow caught him in the side. "Stop calling me that. It sounds weird when you say it."

"Elle?"

"I said stop." She swung at him with her fist. Alan easily caught her hand and pulled her to him. She cried the moment she was in his arms. "Stop being so nice."

"I can't." He rubbed her back.

"Then ignore me."

"I can't."

She tried to push away and took another swing at him. "Yes, you can. You are good at that. I'm quitting. You don't need to pretend anymore."

"I'm not."

"This is stupid. I'm now dreaming of arguing with you and getting a hug. But I need the hug. Today was awful, and I need to pretend for just one more day."

"You're not dreaming."

"Oh yeah? I have to be. You called me Elle, and I didn't like it, and you are holding me, and I can't hit you. But I'm going to wake up." She started crying again.

"Hush, sweetheart."

"You can't tell me to shut up in my dream."

"It isn't a dream. I love you."

"Sweet hot peppers. Don't let this dream end."

"I love you." He kissed the top of her head. By the time she was fully cognizant, the three words wouldn't be as hard to say.

"See, that proves it. You would never say you love me. Next, you will take me out on the lounge chair and hold me so I can sleep without rolling on my arm because that's how this dream goes. Only then, I roll over on the pillow and it hurts because I wake up. I don't want to wake up. I like this stupid dream."

Alan was torn between laughing out loud and scooping ZoElle into his arms and going out onto the balcony. Thanks to the ship's security systems, the balcony was a good choice. Mostly because he knew there was an invisible chaperone with the security cameras. "I like your dream too. Let's go to the balcony."

The light was too bright. Elle turned her head away. The pillow smelled like Alan. It had been a mistake to wear his shirt. She'd spent far too much time dreaming about him last night.

The pillow was solid, not down or foam.

Great, another crazy dream. The prescription must be making her hallucinate. Like the conversation she'd dreamed about when Alan offered to hold her so she could sleep.

Elle's eyes flew open. Four feet poked out from under the blanket. Either she was dreaming she was an octopus or Alan was holding her on the balcony lounge chair.

"Good morning, sleepyhead." Alan's voice vibrated through her.

She swiveled her head, her nose bumping his chin. *Sweet hot peppers.* She tried to sit up, but his arms held her fast. "How did I, I mean, we ...?"

"Do you remember last night's conversation?"

"You called me Elle."

"And you spit fire like a she-dragon."

"You hugged me."

"I didn't want you to hurt yourself."

"I cried."

"Um-hm."

"You said—" No, that couldn't be right. Alan would never have said the three words bouncing around her brain.

"I said I love you."

Sweet hot peppers. Of all the stupid hallucinations.

"ZoElle?" Alan's fingers caressed her chin, then turned her face to him.

"I need to tell the doctor I'm hallucinating."

Alan's chuckle rumbled straight from his chest through hers. "You're not hallucinating. I told you last night I'd keep telling you until you believed me."

"You told me last night?"

"Yes." Alan adjusted his hold so she had a better view of his face—and those eyes. She could literally drown in them. Maybe she had. That would explain what was going on.

"What did I say?"

"Sweet hot peppers. Don't let this dream end."

Elle winced. "Did you kiss me?"

"On the forehead. You were far enough gone that I wasn't sure a kiss would be consensual."

Any kiss, anytime, would be consensual. Only not with morning breath.

Alan searched Elle's eyes. If she hadn't been drowning before, she was drowning now. He chuckled. "You're wondering if you are dreaming again, aren't you?"

"If I was dreaming, my shoulder would feel better."

He ran his fingers down the side of her face. "You have a bruise."

"I got slammed into a wall. I wasn't good enough."

Alan's eyes widened. "What do you mean?"

"Yesterday. I goofed and everything went wrong. I could have gotten us killed."

"You were brilliant. You made a tough call and ended up getting your principal out unharmed."

"But—"

Alan placed a finger on her lips. "No buts. Yesterday didn't go down perfectly. I should have walked you over to Cassie's suite or insisted you turn on your earrings before you left. I shouldn't have sat in the room for an hour like a helpless, lovesick fool doing nothing while a pop can recorded every move."

"Like a what?"

"You heard me." Alan's face reddened.

Elle rested her head against his shoulder, partially to escape the intensity behind his eyes and partially because his words had sent her mind spinning.

Alan's fingers wandered around the edge of her face, leaving little trails of fire. "Go back to sleep. We can have this conversation later."

"Will you still love me then?"

"Always."

Melanie and Cassie came over before noon and sent Alan to go change and shave.

Cassie sat down on the couch. The sparkle had left her eyes. Elle sat down in one of the chairs. "How are you doing?"

"The doctor may not have found any broken bones on me, but everything else feels broken. I can't believe I married him. Peter warned me at Christmas that he didn't like Case. I thought Peter was being Peter. He never likes anyone I date."

Behind her, Melanie shook her head, telling Elle not to pursue the conversation.

"What's worse is the entire country will know some guy pretended to love me for my money. Even with an annulment, I'll always know I saved myself for the wrong marriage. I feel so used."

Elle leaned forward. "I assume you know my history?"

Cassie nodded.

"Nick Gooding, the billionaire, not the creep who tried to kill me, got me the best counselor he could. I loved her. She gave me this analogy: If someone broke into your home and stole your TV, would you replace it?"

"Of course."

"Would you replace the TV with the same old model or the newest one?"

"The newest."

"If someone broke into your car and took your cell phone, would you replace it?"

"Yes. I think I see where you're going with this. The analogy works for you because he did break in and steal…but I opened the door and invited Case in."

"You invited a criminal who had a well-planned heist in mind. He stole a piece of you in the process. Give yourself permission to replace what he stole. It will take awhile. I know. I can call my therapist and see if she can recommend someone in your area. She might do online, but she prefers in person."

"Is she in Chicago?"

Elle nodded.

"I may need to visit Chicago…Dallas may be rather uncomfortable for me for a while. I'd recommended Dr. Johnson join the hospital staff…" Cassie put her head in her hands.

Melanie sat down next to her. "If you come to Chicago, I hope you'll consider staying with Jethro and me. Home is so much better than a hotel."

Elle laughed. "Be warned, their ordinary-looking house is more secure than Fort Knox. Alan claims a cockroach can't move within a thousand yards of the house without them knowing."

"I wouldn't go that far," laughed Melanie, "but your security team will be thrilled."

"After this, dad won't let me go anyplace without a full team for a year. Or ten. At least I talked him out of a helicopter whisking me away. The captain says they can get me off the ship in the morning with no one noticing."

Elle knew she needed to change the subject. "Can you two help me? As comfortable as the T-shirt and sleep pants thing is, I'd like to look more presentable when Alan gets back."

Cassie raised her eyes. "How presentable?"

Elle felt the heat rush to her cheeks. She glanced at Melanie, then back at Cassie. "Presentable enough that Alan thinks of me as a woman and not a broken bodyguard. He wants to take me to dinner."

"Do you want me to leave?" Melanie smiled. She'd be the perfect mother-in-law. Not many women had the opportunity to love their mother-in-law. Elle already did. "I know me being here might be awkward since he is my son, but I'll be honest. I'd like nothing more than to help you knock that thickheaded son off his feet. And I am not talking on the sparring mat."

Obviously, Alan had not filled his mother in on their conversation that morning, which was fine by Elle.

"Do you have any dresses you haven't worn?" Cassie walked in the direction of the closet.

"There are a couple—a green formal and a pink sundress. I would like to try to hide the bandage on my throat."

Cassie peeked around the corner, a real smile on her face. "Trust me?"

Elle nodded only because of Cassie's smile.

"Melanie, I'm going to have Peter take me down to the shops." Elle almost sighed in relief. It would be less embarrassing if she needed help with a shower with only Melanie around.

THE SASSY SENIORS MET ALAN near their favorite gossip spot. Their pink shirts all had big lips and "Kiss me, I'm fabulous" on them. Alan knew they'd worn them just for him.

"Look at that face. He told her!"

"She must not have kicked him to the curb."

"He's in luuvve."

"Look at his blush."

"Hello, ladies." Alan couldn't help but smile at them. "Is everything ready?"

"We've been busy. Macarons. Flowers. Music. Fake candlelight."

"Check."

"Check."

"Check."

Linda beamed. "And the best surprise—when the captain found out what we were planning, he offered a private dining room!"

"How did he find out?" asked Alan.

"Oh, we made a point of finding him and telling him."

"This is like a real-life *Love Boat*!"

"You come on as bride and groom and leave engaged!"

Alan hugged each of the women. "Thank you."

Three hours later, flowers in hand, he knocked on the door of the suite he'd stayed in for the last two weeks.

His father answered the door. For a moment, Alan worried he was going to get a dad lecture. Then Jethro opened the door wide to reveal ZoElle, hair cascading around her shoulders in waves. The light-green dress she wore was one of those special colors women gave odd names to, but it was her sparkling eyes that took his breath away. For the first time in days, even they were smiling at him.

The Sassy Seniors waited at the elevator in matching green shirts. Each presented Elle with a macaron tied up in a little bag.

"Sweets for the sweet."

"Have a good date, kids."

"Whatever he asks, say yes."

"We want photos."

Elle didn't need to look at the stainless-steel elevator door to know she was blushing to the roots of her hair. Her green dress brought out the blush more than it should. Silly complementary colors. The scarf Cassie had purchased for her covered the bandage on her neck and much of the black sling.

Alan let out a nervous chuckle when the elevator doors had closed behind them. "They aren't very subtle, are they?"

"They are adorable. If I had a grandma, I think she'd be like them." Her mother had been forty-five when she'd come along. Her grandparents had all died before she could read.

"They would get you into so much trouble."

"But they'd keep life interesting."

Alan led her through a door marked Private.

Elle paused. "Should we be here?"

"The captain offered. He's more than thankful for what you did yesterday."

"Am I the only one who sees how bad I messed up?"

Alan stopped and turned to face her. "Yup. Because you didn't. Was the rescue ideal and flawless? No. But this wasn't a test at the gym. This was real life, where Colin's latest gadget failed. Ideal decisions can't be made. Injuries happen. Andrew nearly got himself killed last fall, but he saved lives in the process. Please stop being so hard on yourself." He cupped her bruised cheek with his hand. "What you see as a failure, the rest of us see as a win. A lot of bodyguards claim they'll take a bullet for their principal, but few ever do."

He dropped her hand, Elle immediately feeling the loss. A steward opened the door to a small dining room.

"Welcome."

Soft music played, and a table for two sat off to one side of the room near floor-to-ceiling windows.

It was awkward eating with one arm in a sling. The salad wasn't too difficult, but the filet mignon needed to be cut with more than just a fork.

Alan held up his knife. "May I?"

"I hadn't thought eating would be such a problem."

"I should have planned the menu better. I was thinking of your favorites."

"And I have them." Elle offered a tentative smile. "The evening is perfect."

"ZoElle, I mean, Elle—"

She put a hand up to stop him. "ZoElle. Now that you've explained it, I can't bear to have you call me 'her.'"

A smile spread across his face. He slid out of his seat and took a knee. "ZoElle means 'life.'" And that's what you have become. My life. I know you didn't believe me this morning as I explained it over and over. I love you. I have for so long. I just couldn't admit that you're all I need. Marry me?"

Elle covered her mouth. She'd only had an over-the-counter pain pill. Ibuprofen didn't normally cause hallucinations. "You are certain?"

"Yes. Please tell me I didn't take too long to see what was right in front of me."

"No, I mean, yes. I mean, no, you didn't wait too long. Yes, I'll marry you."

Alan stood and pulled Elle into a kiss as the music changed to one of the songs on Abbie's playlist. "Dance?"

"I can't, not with my arm."

"Lucky for me it's an '80s love song. Perfect for the two-step shuffle." Alan held Elle close, and they swayed to the slow ballad. With his arms around her waist and her good arm around his neck, Alan also learned why all the teens in the '80s movies kissed as they danced. The shuffle was made for it.

Epilogue

THANKS TO SOCIAL MEDIA'S HALF-TRUTHS, ZoElle was in the news again. Alan combined his fiancé duties with off the book personal security keeping her newfound fans at bay. Over the last eight weeks things had calmed as other stories hit the news cycle to replace leaked versions and 'eye witness' accounts of ZoElle saving the heiress from her conniving groom.

ZoElle exited the physical therapist's office with an official letter stating she could return to full activity. Alan took the paper from her. "I don't think he understands what full activity means in your case."

"So help me, if you try babying me anymore…"

Alan drew her into a hug and placed a kiss on her nose. "We need to get to the family dinner. Dad has an announcement."

"What's going on? Your parents normally have family dinners on Sundays."

Alan opened the passenger-side door. "I'm not sure. Abbie's hosting, and Andrew and Jordan flew in this morning."

"What gets the whole family together?"

"For the past year, it's been babies and weddings."

Their wedding was still three weeks off. ZoElle wanted to have her surgery far behind her before she walked down the aisle again, especially since they'd planned a mountain getaway for the honeymoon. With all her downtime, she'd had plenty of time to plan the wedding, even inviting the Sassy Seniors, who declined as they were taking a cruise in Norway. Abbie had kept the Mateo-original dress, so that was taken care of too.

ZoElle tapped her chin. "Maybe Andrew and Jordan are apologizing for the elopement. But that's hardly an announcement."

Alan drove through the security gate of the Harmon mansion. The front drive was full of SUVs. "Looks like we're the last ones here."

A butler opened the front door. "Go ahead to the dining room."

With all five grandchildren in highchairs, dinner wasn't the place for an announcement, although Jordan and Andrew apologized for their elopement during every quiet moment.

"Please don't be upset with Andrew. For once in my life, I wanted to do something without the world following me around, and when our plane had to land in Colorado ..." Jordan's sappy grin belied her apologies. She was not sorry at all.

Abbie fed the boy in green another spoonful of something that matched his shirt. "Don't think that gets you out of the ribbing, little brother."

Andrew raised his hands defensively. "We already gave Harmon media an exclusive interview with photos."

Preston took the boy in red out of his highchair and passed him off to a nanny for cleanup. "Considering the deal you cut on publicity for your indie movie, your interview better sell."

Abbie laughed and leaned over to kiss her husband. "Don't be so stern. I already short-sheeted their beds in the guesthouse."

Jordan's jaw dropped, and she turned to ZoElle. "Is it always like this?"

"I've heard all of them say that every day is pick-on-Andrew day. Now that he's left Chicago, I think you'll get this every time you visit."

"Good. I love it!" Jordan's grin was infectious.

Adam rapped on the table with his knuckles. "Harmony would like to say something."

September leaned over and whispered in her daughter's ear. Harmony grinned, her tiny white teeth showing. She used her plastic-tipped spoon to point around the room. "Gamma. Gampa. Unka Alex. Aunt Kimby. Cay." Alex and Kimberly beamed, even though she'd left the *l* out of Clay. "Unka Preston. Aunt Abbie. Naughty boys." Everyone snickered at her reference to Brandon, Connor, and Davis. They weren't even walking and were already causing chaos. They had all tugged on Harmony's hair more than once. "Unka Drew. Princess." Harmony beamed at Jordan.

"Sorry, I let her watch some of your old shows. She loves the title sequence," explained September. "I can't convince her you are Aunt Jordan now."

"Unka Ala, Elle. Daddy, Mamma. Me. Baby." She tossed her spoon at September.

Melanie was the first to react. "What?"

Adam kissed September's cheek. "We are calling him or her Honey."

Kimberly opened her ever-present sketchbook. "Honey the honeymoon baby. Hmm...I can just picture a baby bee."

Alex released Clay from his highchair. "Congratulations, you two. Anyone else with startling announcements?"

Andrew pushed back from the table. "Don't look at us. Our elopement is old news."

"Only news we have is that ZoElle can return to work full-time." Alan caressed the back of her hand.

Jethro leaned forward. "Has she decided which firm she's going to work for?"

ZoElle shook her head. "I've really enjoyed working temp over in the Dermot office, but with Deidre retiring, you need me more, and I can't guard their number-one client." She snuck a look at Abbie. "Conflict of interest, since she is soon to be my sister-in-law."

"Well, maybe we can help you make up your mind after dessert." Melanie gave Jethro the sort of secret look ZoElle hoped Alan would still give her in forty years.

After dinner, the grandchildren were put to bed, and everyone retired to one of the living areas. Everyone looked to Melanie and Jethro.

Jethro stood with Melanie at his side. "After over forty years in the personal-security business, we've decided to retire."

"Take cruises where we don't have to wear toupees," added Melanie. "Spoil grandchildren. Offer unsolicited advice."

"You already do that," said Abbie.

"We made this decision almost two years ago, then Abbie got married, and so we put it off," said Jethro.

Melanie explained with her hands. "By then I was helping September stay in hiding with her pregnancy, and we decided to wait a bit longer because I couldn't turn her case over until she decided to let me tell someone." Everyone looked at Adam.

"We thought we would tell you guys around Mother's Day, but then Alex suddenly married Kimberly, and Abbie was having difficulties with the pregnancy, and then with Deidre working contract for Dermot, we knew we needed another strong female lead and we'd need to wait to get her back. When Elle, I mean ZoElle, sorry dear, I keep forgetting..." Melanie smiled at her soon-to-be daughter in law. "When ZoElle took down one of the men who were after Kimberly, we knew we'd found her. We just needed to get her through training since she had an academic background."

Jethro interrupted. "To be honest, your mom also thought Alan would see what was literally sitting in front of him and make a move and we'd have a Christmas wedding too. We didn't count on Andrew surprising us all."

"Andrew's always been a bit of a surprise," said Abbie behind her hand. Everyone but Andrew laughed.

Jethro cleared his throat. "Anyway, now that Alan knows what's best for him, we think it's time for us to retire. Alan and ZoElle will take over the head-office management. Adam and Alex can stay in their current roles, which will allow them the flexibility to work with their wives' careers. Andrew can still work in California."

"Wait. What about my contract with Dermot?" asked ZoElle.

"Simon kept you as a contract employee at my request. I wanted you to have this choice, and he agreed."

Alan looked from one parent to the other. "Just a minute. You could have used Ben and Tonie on the ship, couldn't you?"

"No. You two were really the best pair for the job."

"Had you not come to your senses, I would have arranged for both of you to be stranded on a deserted island for as long as it took." Abbie grinned.

"Not fair. You started the hasty Hastings reputation by marrying your client." Alan's protests were met by a knowing smile.

"Which I did in a little over a month because I'm smart that way." Abbie kissed Preston until her husband blushed.

"I didn't need that long." Alex hugged Kimberly to him.

She tapped him on the nose. "It took you longer to fall in love with me."

"Nope. I fell in love the moment you pulled the gun on me." Alex gave his wife a kiss as passionate as his twin had given her husband.

Alan rolled his eyes. "I still didn't take as long as Adam."

"Careful there. That's my husband you're maligning. I can write you into a country song you'll never live down." September didn't let Adam respond before kissing him.

Melanie put her hands on her hips. "I never thought I would say this to my children, but some of you need to get a room."

"Gladly." Andrew and Jordan answered in unison.

Jethro crossed his arms and leveled a dad look at everyone. "Back to the matter at hand. We would like to phase ourselves out over the summer. Alan and ZoElle deserve a wedding and a honeymoon before we fully retire."

"Wahoo! Where are you going?" asked Abbie.

ZoElle gave Alan's hand a squeeze. "Not on a cruise."

"And no place you have the address to." Alan kissed ZoElle on the top of her head.

Jethro put an arm around his wife. "I think we lost control of this conversation somewhere along the line."

"I don't think so. I think it ended up exactly the way we wanted it to." Melanie stood on her toes and brought her lips to meet her husband's.

ZoElle hid her blush in Alan's arm. In forty years, she wanted to be exactly where her future in-laws were now.

acknowledgements

FOR FIVE YEARS I'VE BEEN blessed to swim with some of the most amazing women. They have cheered me on since the release of Waking Lucy four years ago, and always ask what I am writing. Several of them go on a cruise or two each year and helped me with some ideas for this story. Also a shout out to my mother-in-law, Pat, who shared with me her knowledge of cruises. Without these wonderful ladies Alan's trip wouldn't have been as fun.

As always, thanks to Tammy, Nanette and Cami who are so willing to help make all my projects better and to read for all my mistakes. I would never make it through a day without Sally and Cindy whose advice keeps me going. Thank you wonderful ladies.

Michele at Eschler Editing does the best edits; any mistakes left in this book are not her fault. Nor are my excellent proofreaders to be blamed. Thank you ladies and gents!

My family, for sharing their home with the fictional characters who often get fed better than they did. And my husband who encourages me every crazy step of the way and puts up with all my messy spreadsheets.

And to my Father in Heaven for putting these wonderful people, and any I may have forgotten to mention, in my life. I am grateful for every experience and blessing I have been granted.

about the author

LORIN GRACE WAS BORN IN Colorado and has been moving around the country ever since, living in eight states and several imaginary worlds. She holds a degree in Graphic Design.

Currently, she lives in northern Utah with her husband, four children, and a dog who is insanely jealous of her laptop. When not writing, Lorin enjoys creating graphics, visiting historical sites, museums, painting furniture and reading.

Three of her books, Waking Lucy (2017), Mending Fences (2018), and Not the Bodyguard's Baby (2020) have won Recommend Read awards in the League of Utah Writers Published book contest.

You can learn more about her, and sign up for her newsletter at loringrace.com or at Facebook: LorinGraceWriter.

The favorite word she's ever written in a book is "decrescendo." She'd love to hear from you if you spot it.

www.ingramcontent.com/pod-product-compliance
Lightning Source LLC
Chambersburg PA
CBHW020836260626
47169CB00003B/1012